ADRIJA
An Unusual Love Story & BEYOND...

A ROMANTIC THRILLER FROM
ROHIT ASHOK KOTHARI

HOL ISTIC Publishing

Published by "The Great Indian Book Tour"
Imprint : Holistic Publishing
www.tgibt.com
106/91, Ashok marg, Vijay path
Mansarover, Jaipur, Rajasthan-302020
Phone : +91-72400-68114
email : prashant@tgibt.com

Title : **ADRIJA**
Author : **ROHIT ASHOK KOTHARI**
Copyright © **ROHIT ASHOK KOTHARI** 2024
All rights reserved

First published in 2024
First Edition 2024

ISBN : 978-93-93262-80-6

INTRODUCTION

This book is dedicated to all the booklovers and readers, who have encouraged me to endure my passion -Writing. Without you, the journey would have been void and there would be no reason for me to pen these narratives and bring them to life. So, thank you for believing and embracing my stories with utmost Warmth & Love.

Also, in the story, I have put efforts to weave a few heroic moments, selected icons and certain places, which play a momentous role in making India what it is. Plus, these cites infuse a sense of pride in each individual (every Indian) and gives us the reason to feel joyous as well as celebrate the glory of our motherland- INDIA.

These (handful) references are an attempt to relive, revive and experience those celebrations and recollect every bit of the past. Furthermore, the story is dedicated to this city- Mumbai, and I have taken this as an opportunity to express my unconditional love for the city that never sleeps.

Last but not the least, this book is for my Family & Friends. Thank you for your unwavering support and being with me in my tough and happy times.

Love-

ROHIT ASHOK KOTHARI

Contents

CHAPTER 1
THE CAB ENCOUNTER
MUMBAI, INDIA

❝The night is turning into a nightmare and there are warnings by the meteorological department for it to get worse. There is water logging seen in all parts of the metropolitan. The water that should ideally be thrown out, is rather getting pushed into the city; all thanks to our failed drainage systems. This showcases the failure of the local civic bodies and exposes the false promises made (by them) for getting into power. None of them want to concentrate on the urban development and rather continue to fill their pockets shamelessly. Everybody is corrupt and nobody cares what a common man feels," addresses Kaushik Avasthi, the prime-time reporter from Today & Now news to his viewers.

"We have Mukund Deshapande on the streets of Mumbai, reporting live from ground level amid this heavy downpour, just for you. Hello Mukund can you hear me?" asks Kaushik with all efforts put in, trying to connect with Mukund.

"Yes Kaushik I am able to hear you," replies Mukund as the sound from the studio reaches his ear-piece.

"Wonderful! So, Mukund you are there live on the streets. Tell me how do you feel and what kind of atmosphere is built around you? What kind of jeopardy is it like? And what are the sentiments of a common man currently?" asks Kaushik from the studio.

"PATHETIC! This is one word that describes it all, Kaushik. There is blue everywhere- on the streets, pouring from up there and elsewhere," replies Mukund screaming his lungs out. He stresses on his talk as the winds along with the rain, make it difficult to speak with every passing moment.

"Absolutely this is unacceptable. Please continue Mukund, our viewers are watching," says Kaushik expressing his dismay from the media center.

"Yes, Kaushik. Let me tell you, moreover, it appears as if there were no land and these skyscrapers were built on the sea. Two hours of heavy deluge and the streets have gone invisible. As per the red alert (by the meteorological department) issued, if this continues for the next 24 hours, with same intensity, then I am worried and it perturbs me even as I speak, the entire city will erode and get whitewashed," speaks Mukund with an irked tone.

"The kind of work done by our 'so-called' local bodies, highly differs from the promises made (before they were elected) and is evident from the current scenario. To be precise, the truth seems to have surfaced, exposing this entire rumpus. The citizens have been fooled yet again and unfortunately this kind of barbarity appears unstoppable," replies Kaushik in fierce tone.

"Kaushik there is a news breaking-in from our sources. There has been a major electric shut-down in various parts of the metropolitan to avoid any unfortunate events. Also, local police and other government officials are forcing us to move from here, as the area is continuously receiving heavy precipitation. So with cameraman Amin Shaikh, this is Mukund Deshapnde for Today & Now news," with this Mukund signs off.

"Thank you Mukund for the live updates. So viewers, our reporters are present at ground level and will keep updating you minute by minute. For now, it is a good-bye time from me- Kaushik Avasthi, keep watching Today & Now news for latest updates. Stay home, stay safe and do not get out from wherever you are, unless necessary. Take care," with this the Today & Now news journalist Kaushik Avasthi leaves.

There were such kind of headlines and breaking news played all over on the television sets, radios, and social media channels. This instilled absolute fear and the situation appeared extra panicky than it actually was. This created additional chaos and situation began to lose hold due to the continuous bombardment of such ruthless media showdown.

However, on the other hand the government officials, policemen and other local civic body officers, tried providing some relief by assuring every kind of help to anyone in need. Also, they constantly posted the goods on the social media- like how people who got stuck were transported to a safer place, safeguarding the stray animals from the peril, constantly flashing helpline numbers to reach out for help and things like those. Along with, these officials requested everyone to stay safe and calm.

All said and done, it was a never seen before experience for the entire city. Breaking all the past records of shower, in a mere span of two hours, the situation had taken every citizen by scare. The entire city appeared to be sinking (rather drowning); furthermore the situation turned more worrisome with every passing moment. More likely because the water was unable to find its way out.

Every resident appeared highly disappointed as there were no prior predictions from the meteorological department of the torrent. Not only this, two-hours ago, the day acted normal with Sun preparing itself for setting down; and the sky viewing beautiful and clear (and of course with no hints of any rainfall). Post sun-set, the climatic conditions took a major turn around and the weather changed dramatically, rather drastically reaching another end of extremity. Usually, Mumbai is known for its heavy-rainfall and every citizen has a ready mindset to take it as it comes every year. But this was beyond crazy. .

9 P. M Mumbai Central station

Slowly and steadily, the electric cut down was implemented in most parts of the city. This had left the streets dark and pitch black. The landscape appeared no less than merciless. It continued to remain relentless with thunderstorm, full-force downpour, and ferocious lightning. The rain God had made the decision to be unstoppable, that too at an impeccable force and unfortunately, the resolution looked irrevocable.

The gusty winds accompanying the rains, had drenched everyone irrespective of the fact, that an individual carried protection or not. Also, the visibility had reduced to less than a meter, adding to the already elated- suffering and woes. The fierce lightning, arising from the pitch-black sky looked frightening and gave jitters to those waiting on the railway platform. Amid all of this, came a news of cloudburst in Thane, that broadcasted like a scare and petrified the passengers and/or others even further.

The water-logging on the railway tracks, led to the delaying of the arrival and departure of trains. This seemed no good to anyone and raised the frustration levels of both- the commuters and those anticipating the arrival of their near and dear ones.

Furthermore, when the eyes turned to the upside direction, there were electric wires entangled like a web. These wires were left exposed- bare and open in the rains- making it a perfect ingredient for every possible mishap, leading to an unforeseen occurrence. Every individual on the platform, wished to get back to a safer place, at the earliest. Every face appeared petrified and eyes conveyed the prayer to the Almighty, hoping to not encounter any misfortune.

Soon, as the digital indicator displayed quarter past nine (9.15 PM), the passengers on platform number 1 could hear the hoot of the arriving train. The incoming locomotive with a halogen bulb as the headlight- was bright enough to illuminate the immediate darkness, but surely not good enough to provide a long-lasting clear vision to the engine driver. As the train neared entering the platform, it turned really slow and constantly honked to beware the ones on the station platform. Finally, after a delay of more than an hour, the train numbered- 111022 arrived and stopped on platform number 1.

From the coach number A-2, alighted a good-looking, wheatish skin toned young man. Having a backpack, medium-size yellow colored luggage bag and an umbrella along. The man had enticing looks like triangle-shaped face, with side-parted hairstyle, wide-forehead, clean-shaven and a braced jawline.

To complement the facial appearance, he had a brown colored rimless eye-gear on. Decked in formal attire: - ink-blue colored pants and white shirt, with tan-brown waist belt (with rose-gold buckle) and shoes harmonized with the belt, enhanced the young man's personality. On the wrist of his left hand, he had worn a tan-brown leather belt analogue wrist watch with rose gold dial (matching the all browns on the body and especially the waist-belt). While, the right hand struggled to get a hold on the umbrella because of the gusty winds blowing.

As soon as he descended, he walked towards the exit. Upon coming out of the platform, finding a local run-away transport in these rains looked impossible. He took out his phone and opened the cab booking app on the device. Slow network and rarity of signal interfered with interface of the application.

After much ado, he was able to enter his destination and keenly waited for results. Finally, the long wait ended and the application showed the availability of the only car. Already, troubled and exhausted, the young man booked the available four-wheeler without any delay.

The linger continued when he was unable to see the arrival of cab even after ten minutes of his confirmed booking. Besides, he was unable to track the live status of the cab, due to unavailability of the consistent internet. Fatigued of the connectivity and bushed by the heavy-pour, he soon called the cabbie, "Hello I am waiting at the arrival pick up, where are you?"

"Sir, I am waiting at the parking lot," came a reply from the other side of the phone, not so clear and crisp. The cab driver continued to speak something but the call got dropped. The young man tried calling over again, but the network continued to descend on the poor side and the conversation never happened.

The last thing heard was at the parking lot. Being devoid of the good visibility and fear of losing out on the last available cab, the man brisk walked towards the parking lot and started searching for the car.

After covering a distance of about 500 meters, it became easy to recognize the booked car from faraway, as it was the only ash-grey colored sedan (amongst all the other white cabs) in the entire parking lot. He kept approaching the car, dragging the luggage-bag with one-hand, and struggling with an umbrella in the other.

Finally, on coming to a distance of less than two feet, he matched the car's number with the number shown on the booking app. On confirmation, he knocked the glass pane. Subsequently, as the glass rolled down, the sight of the inside of the cab took the young man by surprise. The man was shocked to see a female in-charge of the steering inside the cab. This left him perplexed and confused. To double-check on the booking, he went at the boot side of the cab, matched the number and other details of the car with those on his phone.

Every box ticked and there was no fault on the booking part. On ratifying details, he came back, knocked at the closed window yet again. The glass went rolling downwards and, "Are you the driver of the cab?" asked the young man (still appearing very much in shock and confused) to the lady inside.

"Sorry!" came a reply with bizarre expressions and muddled look.

The young man repeated his question, "Are you the driver?"

"Being at the driver's seat and no other human inside the car, what do I look like to you? A bar-tender?" said the taxi-driver furiously and took a short pause. Soon after she continued in awry, "Do not waste time, just hop-in, there is water splashing in the car. Just get in quickly, hurry," came a blunt reply from the lady driver as the window went up.

With this, the young man could not help and against his will, knocked at the window, yet another time. The glass went down once again. But this time around, the cabbie seemed to have lost it completely and with the intense infuriated look she asked," What the hell do you want? Are you seeking for some adventure? Already, I am tired waiting for you, from last 20-25 minutes and you seem to be enjoying the rapid-fire round of questions."

To this the young man innocently replied, "Could you please open the boot? I need to keep the luggage."

"Sure" came a firm reply, as she pressed the button down under her seat, to open the boot.

The young man went at the backside of the car, kept his luggage in the boot and jumped at the backseat. The lady waited for about 10 seconds for the passenger to settle down and post that, "Give number" said the lady turning towards the man.

"What number?" replied the man with an absolute clueless expression.

"OTP?", said the lady in a stressed tone. "I need an OTP to begin the trip. Please give that," came a vexed request from the lady.

"Oh yes! I absolutely forgot. The number is 23984. Sorry, I just missed out, totally," replied the man with a calm smile.

The driver entered the OTP, gave a death stare through the rear-view mirror, and began the trip (finally after all the mess and unwanted gung-ho). The young man ignored the expression (although he very well saw the female getting pissed at him) and began peeping in his phone.

On covering about less than a kilometer, the cab halted at a traffic signal. The lady driver turned her eyes at the navigation map that was set on her phone screen to guide her through the destination. The driver was all agonized and disgusted when the app showed a travel time of about two and half hours. All annoyed she said, "Freak these rains are adding up to the traffic issues and worsening up,".

Getting out of the phone and pretending unknown and unheard, the man said, "Sorry. Did you say something?"

"No. I have a habit of speaking to myself," replied the cabbie in the most taunting tenor.

"My name is Rudra. And yours is?" asked the young man out of nowhere. Taking the conversation to an aimless direction.

"Where did that pop-up from? I am thinking about traffic and you are introducing yourself," asked the cabbie in a baffled tone.

"It is not in your hands, right? You can neither control the traffic nor stop the rains. Then why think? I feel, it will be good if we talk a bit. This might make this ride a bit relaxing for you and may be a memorable one for me," replied Rudra in a very cheery tone.

Rudra sounded weird to the lady, but somehow, she also realized, he was in a way correct. She calmed down a bit and in a peaceful manner said, "Hi. My name is Adrija. And I am sorry for being rude in the beginning."

"Forget the beginning," came an immediate and casual reply from Rudra. He further continued, "Hey that is a beautiful name-ADRIJA. If I may ask you- What does that mean? I have never heard about the same," replied Rudra with all zeal and curiosity.

"Adrija means Mountain Goddess; and is also another name for Goddess Parvati," replied Adrija in a more eased tone.

"I love it. What a profound meaning and how beautiful the name is! Suits you, you beautiful," said Rudra in a frisky manner.

"Excuse me! Are you trying to flirt with me?" questioned Adrija with raised eyebrows, seen clearly through the rear-view mirror.

Rudra made an eye contact through the mirror and immediately denied saying, "For now I don't intend to. But if you wish to, then let me know, I can think of the same."

Adrija ignored the reply and concentrated on driving. All the silence in the atmosphere somehow did not go down that well with Rudra and he budged asking, "You appear very young like a collegian or something. Correct me if I am wrong, but mostly I feel I am not."

"Yes, I am pursuing my Bachelor's degree in Pharmaceuticals and am into my final year. And just before you bombard me with another question- how come I landed in driving. Let me tell you- I am from Bihar and my family is not that financially sound, so to not burden the family back home, I earn and look after myself in all aspects."

Rudra was moved with Adrija's answer and was flattered by her hard-working skills. Though he was not connected to her by any purpose, but her independent nature, gave Rudra, a sense of pride and felt her courageous character was inspiring enough.

The answer touched the soft part of his heart and Rudra got emotional. This had his eyes moist. Hiding the same, soon he got back to his jolly good behavior and said," I am highly impressed and inspired. Wow....! We need more women like you in today's world. Cheers to the women empowerment."

And, Adrija smiled for the very first time looking at Rudra. She saw it all – how Rudra was touched on hearing her, how he turned emotional and how hard he tried to hide his feelings (although failed) and chose not to speak his heart out. She saw it all and ignored immediately, exactly how Rudra wanted.

Showing the intent for the very first time and carrying the conversation forward, Adrija asked, "Are you coming down to Mumbai for the first time?"

"No, I keep coming down for business purpose. But this is for the very first time that I have encountered a female taxi driver. And the experience has been pleasant so far," replied Rudra with a friendly smile.

To which Adrija blandly replied," Okay."

There was absolute silence once again; but this time around, Rudra was mesmerized by Adrija's beauty. As the car had a long halt at the traffic signal, Rudra had enough time to gaze at the ethereal attractiveness that Adrija possessed. She had a round shaped face with a stylish modern-shag haircut (for her full curly hair), perfectly suiting her persona. She was fair, had a perfect button-shaped nose, natural pink bow-shaped lips, sharp jawline, and the most captivating part- were her blue eyes (somehow Rudra was able to notice the eye-color, as she often gave him death stare through the rear-view mirror). The total black uniform (of the cab company) added to the alluring personality. Rudra was blown away and could not help, but continued to stare at her beauty (but in a good away).

As Rurda's eyes continued to appreciate the prettiness that she possessed, Adrija suddenly said," The rains have slowed down a bit and the traffic too is clearing up. Also, the travel time has now come down to less than 90 minutes. You were right Rudra, about not getting irritated and the conversation part, both seem to have worked."

On hearing her, Rudra came out of the dreamy world and in a sulked tone replied, "Yeah, it surely did."

"What! Are you not happy? You must be tired and I am sure there must be something important for you to catch up," replied Adrija on getting a low reply from Rudra.

Rudra had a moment of silence and did not turn up with any reply. On the contrary, Rudra was not happy on the decreased travel time, as it meant- less time to be spent with Adrija. Somewhere, Rudra had started liking Adrija and wanted to know more about her. Also, he knew that this travel time, was his only opportunity to exchange feelings.

On not getting to hear from the ever talkative Rudra, Adrija repeated herself, "Hello, Mr. Rudra, I am talking to you."

Rudra came back to reality on a repeat nudge from Adrija and, "Yes off-course I am happy." He completed his sentence rather short and put a full-stop.

Though he agreed with Adrija on happiness part, but his audio and video did not match. As in, his spoken words indicated a different story than what was evident from his facial expressions. Adrija immediately could sense something not right, but cared the least and continued her duty.

Not continuing to feel sad, Rudra soon turned positive, took the remaining time as an opportunity, and said, "So don't you feel unsafe driving this late and especially under such extreme weather conditions. I mean I know every day counts, but isn't this a bit risky?"

"Every moment lived is risky. Traveling by train is risky. You sitting alone with me is equally risky. You going for meetings and investing in some business is risky. If you walk in these rains, encounter an open electric wire, then it is not only risky but can be lethal and life taking too. If there is so much risk in every bit, then why should only I fear of anything?" replied Adrija in the most straightforward manner as she could, presenting a resilient as well as blithe side of hers.

"Are you usually this outspoken and blunt, or is it me the special one to witness this facet of yours?" asked Rudra in the most ironic pitch he could.

"Well, it is your lucky day. You should be thanking God on experiencing the vicious side of mine," gave back Adrija in a likewise satirical manner.

Rudra understood one thing- Adrija was a tough nut to crack and it was nowhere possible to do so within the stipulated time of ride. But he even knew, he could no way ask for any personal contact; as Adrija was not inn for any kind of light-hearted conversation. Rudra soon realized, it was not his day today. The beginning of this entire thing (which began between the two since the time Rudra approached the taxi) did not take place on a right note, so things that followed continued in the same pattern.

"Could you please play some music?" requested Rudra, as he realized not speaking any further, being the best option.

"Sure, why not? You have paid for the ride and every service that machine can offer is covered under the same. So why not, here you go," and Adrija was at her nasty best. She turned on the music system and the song started, "Kesariya tera ishq hai piya" from the movie Brahmastra.

The song was immortal. As the song continued in the background, it disconnected Rudra from the current fracas. The charismatic melody of the composer and the soulful voice of the singer, took him to another world, radiating a feeling of timelessness and all adoration. This made Rudra feel elated, immersed, engrossed and he visualized himself at a paradise (of course not without his recent crush Adrija).

As the song completed, the end got Rudra, back to actuality and gathering guts he tried initiating the dialog, yet again, "This is one of my favorite films. Have you seen this movie?" asked Rudra. "Please be kind and gentle in answer. Let us not throw tantrums at each other and try behave amicably," pleaded Rudra.

"Okay. Yes, I have seen this movie and kind of loved it too," replied Adrija.

As Adrija for the very first time sounded convincing, Rudra breathed light. It was a sign of hope for Rudra and seeking this as an opportunity, he further continued, "Loving the film meant, even you believe in the power of love. Correct?"

"And what makes you conclude this?" asked Adrija instantly.

"The movie is all about love. Isn't it? The belief that love can conquer anything in the universe, is what makes it special and is also the message in the movie," replied Rudra within no time.

"Well, I loved it for its visual appearance, the cinematic extravaganza, the directors filming acumen and top of all the portray of characters. Yes, off course the message of love was in the movie, but that was the least that reached out to me," replied Adrija straight away contradicting on what Rudra felt about the movie.

And Rudra was back to square one. He did not know any more methods to make Adrija chat and take this tit-bit bickering kind of thing, to a proper some kind of relationship (be it at least friendship or something which would be more amiable).

The other songs continued to play in the background and the time passed. There were no any further conversations between the two. Rudra had given up after trying for every possible notion. For the rest of the journey Rudra did nothing, but gazed at Adrija through the rear-view mirror. Adrija on the other hand was unmoved and concentrated on her job as she did with other passengers, when on board.

As the ETA to the destination showed about 5 minutes, Rudra abruptly burst-out saying, "Look Adrija, I tried having a healthy conversation with you but unfortunately it crash-landed every time. I want to know more about you and looking forward to meet you again. I do not know how, but I certainly wish to."

To this Adrija replied rather quickly, "I was just kidding about the reasons I gave for liking the movie. The main reason for me to love the film was- the portrayal of power of love in the best possible way."

Rudra appeared enigmatic and perplexed. He found it really weird of Adrija's reply and with all apprehension said, "I am sharing my feelings here and you are commenting on film's likeability. I hope you get what I am trying to convey."

"I totally get it and care about your feelings; which is why I gave you the real reason and changed my answer about the movie. C'mon Rudra ji put some pedal on the intellect and accelerate your thinking system. We are running short of time," replied Adrija in a jovial tone.

The ETA reduced to 3 minutes and Rudra appeared blank. He closed his eyes and in his mind, played a recap of the conversation that happened between the two in regards to the movie. And soon he realized what Adrija meant. Opening his eyes, excited he said, "I cannot believe it. You too indirectly hinting at liking me? See I told you this ride might turn out to be a memorable one for me."

"I like your company and the fact that you do not give up on things easily, is exactly my kind of a thing. I would also like to catch up with you but how is the question. Because you reside outside Mumbai and I am a full time Mumbaikar for the past 4 years," replied Adrija.

"Coming down to Mumbai from Pune is just a 4 hours' drive, so that is not going to be a problem at all. The real difficulty is not having your contact. So, it will be helpful if you can share your number with me," replied Rudra electrifyingly.

"Well, I refrain from sharing my contact. I do not want my phone to be bombarded with messages and calls, as I entirely wish to concentrate on my career. As I told you about my financial background, you can understand how much cutting down from this elusive world is important for my future," replied Adrija in a dismayed tone and appeared disappointed.

And with this the car stopped. Rudra realized he had reached the destination and the trip had come to an end. Along with the trip, the hope of meeting again seemed blurred and negative.

Rudra, just before getting down said, "I understand your career-oriented attitude and do not feel bad about the same. But I am disappointed with you giving a hope of reunion and the very next moment shutting all doors of its possibilities."

Turning her face at the back from the driver's seat, Adrija replied with a smile on her face, "We want to meet, so there must be a way out; and which is why I encouraged the feelings. You can give me your number and can take my hostel's contact. Inform me about your arrival well in advance and this is how we can catch up. Got it?"

After a short pause, Adrija continued, "You are optimistic when it comes to approaching something but, get hurt way too easily if it does not turn up your way."

And finally, Rudra had a big smile on his face. Without any delay the two exchanged numbers and he got off the cab. As the rains had come to a halt, Adrija too got off the cab and offered help to Rudra by opening the boot.

Rudra and Adrija for the first time had an eye contact and in no time were hypnotized. Neither of them moved for the next 30 seconds, until there was a buzz on Adrija's phone of the next pick-up.

With this Rudra unloaded his luggage and as Adrija started walking after closing the boot, "Adrija it was nice meeting you and until we meet next," said Rudra offering a handshake.

Adrija took a pause of few seconds, thought and accepted the gesture. This took Rudra's confidence to next level and Adrija got back to the driving seat with a smile. Rudra with a smile, knocked at the window with an intent to remind her the beginning of all this (like he did before the ride started). Adrija reacted positively, understanding the very bit of his intention and getting the glass down this time she smiled, waved, and left.

Surely this meet had turned out to be productive and beguiling for the two. Mumbai rains are known for these kinds of pleasant encounters. There is romance in the air when you are here at this (monsoon) time of the year. One cannot be left disappointed, if somebody tries or wishes with full heart and all determination. The relationship had just begun to bloom and in the early stages; and surely about to entice the two equally with its fragrance.

CHAPTER 2

THE UNOFFICIAL DATE

Evening 7 P. M

On one hand, where Rudra had fallen for Adrija and it was kind of love at first sight for him; Adrija on the other, liked him as a human and enjoyed his camaraderie.

It was Rudra's undying spirit and endless efforts that made Adrija's heart melt. Thus it was more than half the job done (is what Rudra felt). It would not be wrong to say- that the chances of the two coming together in a relationship were high and the failure of this not turning affirmative, were shallow.

After a long wait of over four weeks, the day of meet-up was near (this is what Rudra thought). Rudra again had planned his (Business trip) visit to Mumbai and as stated by Adrija, he thought of informing her well-in advance. Rudra picked up the receiver of the telephone in his living room, dialed the Bombay Girls Hostel's number and waited for the response from the other side.

The phone kept ringing but went unanswered for the first time. This left Rudra a bit disappointed. Hoping to hear from someone, he dialed for the second time. The phone rang and was missed subsequently on the trot.

This made Rudra feel miserable and the negatives had overshadowed the expectations. The gleam of hope soon converted into gloomy cloud. And pessimism begun to pour the unwanted (but may be true) thoughts like- is the number correct? Did she really mean to what she said? Was she very much interested in me that day, or did she just try to make me feel better? Possibly the number is correct but the phone lines were down? And so and so forth.

Dejected and disheartened he dialed again. He had little or no hopes of someone picking up and waited with a dropped face. Suddenly, out of nowhere he heard, "Hello Bombay Girls Hostel, warden Fatima here," somebody finally answered the call.

Rudra jumped out of delight and his happiness knew no limits. All thrilled and getting back the zeal in his voice he replied, "Hi Madam, can you connect the phone to the final year pharma student Adrija."

"May I know who is on the other side of the call? If not urgent then you can share the message with me. I will convey the same to her," said Fatima, firmly.

"I need to talk to the person, privately. I am her family friend," said Rudra.

"Sir it is raining heavily and very difficult to call the student from the other wing of the campus. I request you to please share you message with me or call tomorrow," said Fatima appearing vexed in tone.

"Fatima ji its urgent. Somebody from our family circle is hospitalized and very serious. They wish to see Adrija for one last time," replied Rudra realizing that Fatima was about to disconnect.

"Oh ok. I am sorry sir. In that case, I would want you to call again after ten minutes. I will ask Adrija to be here," replied Fatima in a mellowed tone.

"Thank you, Fatima ji. But you will pick the call up? Right? Before this, I tried twice but it went unanswered and you know how serious this affair is?" asked Rudra to be rest assured.

"Sir, I very well understand. But, to pick the call I need to keep it first. The more you stretch the conversation, the more difficult it will be for me to call Adrija, because the rains are increasing with every passing moment," said Fatima in a repelled tone, already being troubled by the weather.

"Sorry," and with this he kept the call. Fatima on the other hand, herself went to the other wing and then to Adrija's room to inform the seriousness of the matter. Adrija was shocked on hearing the news. Instantly, without any delay, she joined Fatima on her way to the telephone lounge of the hostel.

Adrija walked in the corridor and waited for the call with baited breath. She was unable to overcome her qualms and perspired out of anxiety. A wait of few minutes appeared elongated and forever.

"The man told you he will call back, right? Are you sure madam," asked Adrija, as it was over 15 minutes and the phone had not rung.

"The man asked me to assure if I would have Adrija here for conversation. He appeared hysterical and sounded keen to have a word with you," replied Fatima.

To this Adrija just nodded and continued the indispensable walk. Finally, the phone rang. Adrija ran from the other side of the lounge and gasping she said, "Hello. Who is in the hospital? What happened? Hello."

"Continue to be shocked. It is me, Rudra. I had to lie because your warden was reluctant on having you over the call. I am coming down to Mumbai day after and which is why I called up," replied Rudra.

"Shit! When did that happen and why did you not tell me this before. It is too late of you to inform me about this. But, I will still try to manage," replied Adrija.

On hearing her reply, Rudra appeared confused and could not distinguish if she sounded serious or was in the character so that she could not be doubted by the warden. "Are you denying the meet? Please do not. It was a last-minute meeting for me too, so could not help but inform you this late," pleaded Rudra.

"Send me the visiting hours. I will not be able to make it up tomorrow but will try for day after. I need to talk to my dean and Fatima mam. Wait for my call tomorrow," replied Adrija infusing some clue and hope in Rudra.

"Ok day after at Bandra. The Red Café, Bandstand at 5.30 pm. Please turn up with a positive response," said Rudra stressing on the meet part.

"I will try and inform you with yay or nay tomorrow by 1 p.m. Bye," and with this she hung up. Rudra could sense her intent, but at the same time understand her helplessness.

After the conversation, Rudra just prayed for this meet to happen. All Rudra could do was- wait with all anticipation keeping his fingers crossed. Adrija too at the hostel appeared excited. At the back of her mind, she also feared a denial from the college dean; as it was seeking permit at a relatively short notice. She was not worried about Fatima because she had heard it all and already offered sympathies.

The night passed. The next day just before the beginning of the lecture session, Adrija paid a visit to the dean's cabin. After having a nearabout 10 minutes' discussion with the Dean, she straight went to the telephone lounge. She dialed Rudra's number and to her surprise he picked it up in half the ring, "That was quick. It seems you were sitting next to the phone," said Adrija.

"Yay or nay, is all I want to hear," replied Rudra with his fingers crossed.

"I will be there at the hospital. Please convey my message to uncle," replied Adrija with no expressions on face as Fatima was right next to her, having her ears over the conversation.

On hearing the response, Rudra was elated and felt euphoric. He punched his fist in the air out of delight and said, "I am speechless. Thank you for accepting the invite at such short notice. See you tomorrow."

"Okay," replied Adrija and hung up with a poker face. As she left and reached a distance unnoticeable to Fatima, she too felt happy and appeared excited for the meet.

Adrija reached her room and took out the cell phone from her pocket. Scrolling down, opened the chat application YourBuddy, went to personal chat box of her dad, and started typing-

Hi dad,

I want to share something important with you. I am so happy to inform you that I have met a guy named Rudra who is cute and nice. The way I met him for the first time was not that great but, now looking forward to this second chance. I will be meeting him tomorrow and want to know what destiny has in store for me. I am nervous, yet thrilled and update you once I have finished the meet. Keep blessing and take care.

PS- **Please don't overthink or get upset. It is just a casual meeting.**

And this was it. Adrija soon finished messaging and got back to her regular routine. The day passed by like any other day and the upcoming one, was waited with all eagerness by Adrija & Rudra, both.

THE NEXT DAY-

Talking about Bandstand, one of the most loved places in Mumbai- it is a sea-side walking and jogging boulevard with a cemented esplanade. It also has a parallel ledge that allows people to sit and experience the sundown and enjoy the sea breeze. It is beautifully decorated with proportional setting of trees on the other edge of the esplanade and a fencing that separates it from the busy traffic on the streets.

Rudra had decided to catch up at Bandra Bandstand's- The Red Café. It was one of the iconic cafes of Bandra (A highlight on the opposite side of the avenue) and known as the first post-Independence Indian coffee shop. Known not only for the flavorsome and amazing coffee, but also for its exquisite set-up.

Painted in all white inside-out, the look appeared soothing to the eyes. Lit by the warm-white spot LED lights all over, the luminosity added to the visual appeal of the café. The wooden finish table and metallic (Tri) colored chairs aligned in the C-Shape setting, beautifully complimented the décor.

Apart from the interior and set-up, the most captivating part about this café were the walls, that had some great stories to tell. They had stories of the great Indian achievers like those of-

- *Bhagat Singh-* As a prominent member of Hindustan Socialist Republican Association group and his contribution to the Independence.

- *Swami Vivekananda-* A philosopher, an author and religious teacher. His contributions to the Indian ideologies and society. The reason behind calling him The Father of modern Indian Nationalism; and being credited for raising interfaith awareness.

- *Sardar Vallabhbhai Patel-* A widely celebrated Indian freedom fighter and one of the greatest Indian Independence

Nationalist. A great patriot, great administrator and above all a great human- a rare combination and a man with great vision.

- *Dr. Babasaheb Ambedkar-* One of the architects of the Indian Constitution. A well-known political leader, Buddhist activist, philosopher, anthropologist, and historian. Also, one of the greatest socio-political reformists.

- *Dr. A. P. J. Abdul Kalam-* 'The Missile Man of India'. Dr. Kalam was one of the greatest scientists that India ever had. Also, he was elected as the 11th president of India. A great man at heart, he was a visionary and moreover very clear in his thoughts of what India should look like.

Their journeys were beautifully carved (in detail) on the walls of this café and gave an absolute nationalistic feeling. The ideology behind naming it as The Red Café- was to give a tribute to the blood of the great Indian freedom fighters and political leaders who contributed for the soil.

Talking about its outside seating arrangement- it were modern and atypical than the inside. It had large black colored cantilever umbrellas placed in linear fashion. Underneath the umbrella were wooden table and red colored chairs with seating only for two. This entire set-up was well arranged on a four level of step like parallel arrangement, to provide the sea-view to all the customers seated outside.

Rudra had arrived 15 minutes early and reserved the table for two. Sharp at 5.30 PM, he saw Adrija getting off the auto-rickshaw and his eyes were fixed on the scene.

Adrija wore a sleeveless medallion-yellow polka dot one-piece that went till the knee. She had kept those curls (hair) open and put brown shades, enhancing the aura of hers. The cherry-red lipstick contrasting the attire (as it was meant to), appeared bold & loud, emphasizing on her fearless character. As she walked towards the café, she appeared more and more stunning with every step forward. Lastly, she reached and took the seat. Rudra could not help but continue to gaze at the all glitz and shining Adrija.

"Stop staring at me I am right here," said Adrija as she shied.

Rudra arose out of the fantasy world and replied, "I cannot help because you look jaw-dropping gorgeous. I am enticed and inveigled. I have never seen this beautiful girl in my entire life."

"C'mon Rudra don't try these cheesy one liners at me. Now that I am here, let's order something. I am starving," replied Adrija.

"I swear on my heart; you are the most good-looking girl I have ever met. Anyways, let us order first and then take this evening forward. Coffee? Hot or Cold? And something to munch? By the way sandwiches are great here," replied Rudra, unable to take his eyes off Adrija.

"You know the best food here! How many girls have you dated before me and got to the same place?" asked Adrija with her eyebrows raised and in all suspicion.

"I haven't dated any. It's just that I often come here for meetings with my clients. Can we please order? Even I am feeling the hunger now!" replied Rudra without any hiccups.

Adrija rolled her eye-balls and gave the ambience a look. She could not believe on Rudra's remark, as the place did not suit for any formal meeting. Differing from what he said and without stretching the not-so important conversation further, "Ok. Sure then order what's best, I leave it to you. And yes I would love to have Frappuccino with munchies."

Rudra placed the order and was back to peeking at Adrija without a blink.

Seeing this Adrija said, "Ok! I don't think you are going to initiate a conversation. So let me start with one."

She continued in her typical raised eyebrow avatar, "May I ask- Why did you choose this place for a mere coffee?"

"Before I answer this, I just want to tell- that your eyes talk a lot, rather they warn too much. It gives an impression as if they come with a disclaimer- mess with me at your own risk," replied Rudra instantly.

"Was that a compliment or are you coming harsh at me, like the day you were in the cab," asked Adrija in a wary tone.

"Well, no memories of that day. It was a hell of a day. The only thing to be carried forward from the past are those last 15 minutes. They were beautiful; and are imprinted all over my heart. And which is why I have you here," replied Rudra in the most affectionate way he could.

"Oh! Someone is suddenly turning romantic. You then also remember to what I said- I like your company and nothing beyond for now. Right!" asked Adrija with a cautious sentiment.

"I do. But there is a space of this budding forward, as you yourself just admitted by saying in the end 'for now'. That means there is space of this getting converted. If not more, then I will take this as a 50-50 scenario," replied Rudra confidently.

"My God! This is what I love about you and why I wanted TO MEET YOU AGAIN. You are damn stubborn, although for good and never quit," replied Adrija with a sparkling smile. To this Rudra just shied and felt silence to be better than words.

"Ok coming back to why I chose this location. Just look at the setting," said Rudra pointing towards the sea on the other side of the street.

"Ok I can and what exactly do you want me to see?" asked Adrija.

"See it through your heart and not through the eyes. The vision of INFINITY. The stunning sight of- Sea meeting the Sky, which is (no true) just a MIRAGE (an illusion). The ever calm SEA, embracing the all radiating SUN up in the amber coloured sky; it gives you the feeling of hope, togetherness, selflessness and lot more. The landscape is so picture-perfect," said Rudra getting into the depth of the picturesque.

"Well, I didn't know there is a philosophical side to your personality too," said Adrija on being surprised at how he denoted the setting.

"It is not true and I am not any philosopher. But just look at the view-even the heartless would have their hearts pumping! Moreover, fix your ear-drums on the sound of the waves hitting the rock and those oscillating to & fro. The cool breeze kissing your cheeks and brushing through the hair, anybody would want to close the eyes and feel it. And with this entire mesmeric backdrop, a beautiful blue-eyed girl sitting right in front of you. Wow! The feeling is SURREAL," said Rudra appearing totally lost in the moment.

"Hello, hold on and apply some brakes to the emotional ride of yours. From start you have put the top gear and speeding in with all possible tricks in your armor. Are you trying to spice up this meet or by any chance putting extra efforts and making yourself appear unrealistic," asked Adrija by posing herself as a speed-bump to Rudra's emotive drive.

"Spice-up? Seriously? It is too of a brashy term for this converge. You can call this as a flawless situation for the two of us. A circumstance, that will act as a step closer on the journey- from being we to US. And this is me. When it comes to love, I am even more romantic than the King of Love himself- SRK, who very well is part of this setting. Just look behind," and Rudra asked Adrija to turn as he pointed to Mr. Shah Rukh Khan's Bungalow.

"I know that. And if this is the real you, then I would like to admit that I am flattered with the kind of vision you have for things. How you make nature relatable with one's feeling and that too this beautifully," replied Adrija with all positivity and letting herself relaxed.

Rudra took the compliment with a smile. And with this, the order had arrived. The two pounced on the food as if hungry since years.

As craving settled a bit, "Well, as stated you keep doing meetings here in Mumbai. But I don't know yet, what exactly you do?" asked Adrija.

"Well, you never asked me," replied Rudra in a jovial tone.

"This sounds so kiddish and formal. Ok, I am asking you now- tell me Rudra ji what do you do?" asked Adrija giggling.

"Haha I like this- Rudra ji. I have heard it for the first time. I am often called Rudra sir but this Ji-thing is special to me. So Adrija Ji, I am a contractor by profession. And I…".

"Oh CONTRACTOR! This is why you have brand on all kind of things you wear," Adrija had cut Rudra's reply mid-way. And she continued in a cocky tone, "Big people, big business and bigger brands." Finding her own joke funny, Adrija burst out laughing.

As she continued laughing, Rudra could sense her happiness and he could see the oomph in her eyes. She was unstoppable and Rudra so wished for her to continue.

After a laugh riot of almost 10 minutes, Rudra asked, "So who all are there in your family? I mean don't mind but, I did not have anything to ask, so thought of this being the best way to begin with."

"It was not that great of a start. But now that you have asked I will come straight to the point. I just have my dad to call as family. My mom separated long back, nor do I have any siblings. So it's just me and my Dad," replied Adrija in a firm voice.

"I am sorry for the same. I didn't intent to make this conversation awkward or painful for you," replied Rudra feeling the guilt deep inside.

"Don't be, I am not. It's ok," said Adrija.

Rudra felt bad as he ended up striking the wrong note with his premier question. He did not have courage to pitch any other questions or ask anything more about Adrija. He concentrated on the sandwich and continued to sip coffee, refraining any eye contact with her.

On seeing this Adrija said, "Oh c'mon! You don't need to feel bad about anything. Cheer up and smile."

To this Rudra literally just smiled and nothing beyond. He was still mum and didn't utter at all.

"I am not used to this side of you. Remember the day we met, how much did you question. As if I was taken in a custody or something," said Adrija, trying to push Rudra to be himself.

"Yes I do. I am like this. I love to talk. Moreover, I have been wanting to be in a relationship and then I saw you. It is not that I am desperate or something, but was in search of a right partner. And…" saying this Rudra suddenly paused and looked in to the beautiful eyes of Adrija.

Adrija could see his heart through his eyes. She too appeared to melt with Rudra's innocent approach, "And… Continue. I want to hear what you felt like."

Rudra gathered all his guts and continued, "And then it was love at first sight. I mean you remember my reaction on you opening the window for the first time?"

"Yes I do," replied Adrija with a smile recollecting the incident.

"Frankly I was not surprised seeing a female driver inside. I was rather shocked to see such a beautiful girl at the driver's seat. I had fallen for you at the very moment the glass went down. Your appearance came like a bright ray of sun and the glow of your face was evident even in those heavy rains; despite rarity of clear vision," replied Rudra expressing his heart out.

Adrija blushed. She was kind of moved with the purity with which Rudra felt about her. Plus, how passionately he approached her for everything. Adrija surely had developed feelings for Rudra, but wanted to be sure on the personality part of his. She wanted to be sure if this was the real him. At back of her mind, Adrija was in a dilemma- whether to go with the flow or be a little resistant.

As she continued to fight thousand thoughts in her mind and put efforts to figure out the right passage, Rudra intervened- "Hello miss. I am right here but you seem to be lost somewhere. Is everything okay?" asked Rudra.

"Yes off course, just enjoying the view with delicious food," replied Adrija coming back to the real-world.

And the two continued to enjoy their meal. As they carried on, the beautiful evening turned even more fine-looking. The moon was up in the sky. The full moon had brightened the black (sky) with its radiance and the sparkling stars disseminated all over, enhanced the glow. The reflection of the entire sky on the sea-water felt like the sheet of stars being spread on water, with moon being the highlight.

As they finished the meal, Adrija said pointing at the boulevard, "Can we go for a 15 minutes' walk there. I still have time and would like to be around you."

Rudra was touched on hearing this. And without any delay he agreed. The two got up and went on the opposite side of the street. Adrija enjoyed the setting as she walked through the esplanade, while Rudra cherished his extra minutes with Adrija.

After a silence of about five minutes, Adrija suddenly began to speak, "It feels like I have come across this setting before."

"Sorry. I didn't get you," replied Rudra as he appeared confused.

"I feel as if I have lived this moment before. The sea-side walk, the sound of waves hitting the shore, the walk on the full moon day. It feels like this has happened to me before. I don't know why, but this feels like a repeat from the past," continued Adrija as she perspired and felt perturbed. She appeared distressed and anxious.

"Relax. It happens. These kind of things are called as déjà vu. Need not take this too heavily, let's sit and relax for a while," said Rudra as he tried calming her down.

They sat on the bench, nearby. Rudra held Adrija's hand and tried calming her down. She felt better and slowly began to regain her composure. From then on there was absolute silence. For the next ten minutes, the two continued gazing at the stars with the music of the waves in the backdrop.

"It's time for me to leave, Rudra," said Adrija breaking the silence.

"Are you feeling alright now? I am not letting you go unless you absolutely okay," said Rudra out of concern.

"I am fine Rudra. Thanks for the help and thank you for comforting me. I don't know what happened to me, all of a sudden. Felt like some panic attack or something. But anyways thank you," replied Adrija with a smile.

"Do not use such heavy terms for this mere déjà vu kind of a feeling. Just go back and relax," said rudra trying to instil goodness. To this Adrija just smiled with all heart.

"Time just flew in a jiffy. I am happy to meet you again and would want this something to continue further," continued Rudra on not believing that it was time for Adrija to depart.

"I don't know how to express but would want to confess that I too loved the evening spent with you and would want to carry this forward. And yes you were right, this can convert in to something but I will wish not to rush for now," replied Adrija in a mellowed tone and expressing a little bit of herself.

On hearing the statement, Rudra felt ecstatic. His ears could not believe what was just stated by Adrija. He felt on top of this world and so wished to hug Adrija and express whatever ran through his mind. However, somehow Rudra tamed the over-excited him and barred himself from doing anything over-the-top. On the contrary to the current emotion (that encapsulated his mind) with a plain smile he said, "Thank you and I feel lucky to hear that."

"I will give you one more moment of relief. Next time when you plan to come, just text me on my number. Just that and nothing else. I don't want my inbox to flood. And yes please try to inform a week before," continued Adrija, simultaneously sharing her private number.

"Ok. If I wish to talk? Is there any option to dodge Fatima and directly connect with you?" asked Rudra with some hope.

"Please don't and especially don't kill people for meeting. I did not like the excuse. I know you were exposed to a never witnessed before kind of a scenario, so it is ok this time. Also, talking over call might not be possible but I will try calling you when no one around. Nothing guaranteed! But assure you to meet in person whenever you come down to Mumbai," replied Adrija infusing some positivity with conditions applied.

Rudra nodded without any choice. He offered Adrija to join on her way back to hostel, but she refrained. Adrija stopped a runaway auto and just before she got in, "Until we meet again," she offered a handshake to Rudra.

Rudra smiled and shook hands with her. Soon she left and both were all smiles.

These encounters continued for a period of six months. As they kept meeting often, they got to know each other better and soon just a meet-thing began to shape in a cemented relationship. The proximity increased and the urge to spend more time together, developed. So much that over a period, Adrija began to request Rudra to come down from Pune (especially for the two to meet). Adrija by now had got comfortable in the relationship, however neither had made it official or took an initiative to propose, nor they declared to have dated. They just went with the flow.

CHAPTER 3

THE EERIE ENCOUNTER & THE MEMOIR

One fine day, Morning 5.30 A. M-

Like any other day, Adrija arrived at Aarey colony for a walk. It is still very dark and being winters, the Sun is not seen to rise anytime soon. It is foggy and the visibility is minimal, rather close to negligible. Being a jungle zone, the area felt cooler than what other parts of the city are supposed to be. The digital display at the entrance exhibited a temperature of 10 Degree Celsius, which indicated a record low temperature of the season this year.

Mumbai hardly has any winter and today being one of those lucky days, Adrija is beaming, all thrilled and loving the weather. She is in her typical jog-avatar with jumpsuit on, music being played in her phone and connected with the ear pods. She seemed to enjoy the setting. Adrija usually met other health freaks at this early time of the day during her workout session, but today none seem to be present (possibly because of the cold weather).

Least bothered about the absence of others, Adrija began brisk walking. With every step forward, she appeared to fall in love with the wonderful weather. Slowly and steadily, Adrija began to gain some pace and soon switched to jogging.

After a run of almost 10 minutes, she began to put in extra efforts against the winds that suddenly began to blow. The air propelled in the opposite direction (as that of Adrija) and the intensity increased with every passing minute. Soon the force reached a point which made it difficult for Adrija to tear apart the air blanket. She not only felt difficulty in running but breathing had also become a task, compelling her to pause.

As she stood in the mid of the forest in all dark and alone, Adrija felt terrible. The perfect setting of the winter morning that Adrija enjoyed a while ago, all of a sudden looked scary and made her feel somewhat uncomfortable.

The gushing wind colliding with the bushes (of the trees) created an abnormal sound. The cry of the owl, the howling of the animals and the background noise like these, added to the scenario of this black and creepy milieu. Adrija began to shiver and sweat (not due to jogging) purely because of the spooky-like situation building around her.

Adrija appeared petrified and continued to feel terrible. She took a glance and wished if she could reach someone for help; but failed to find any human in this entire jungle. And top of all- the environment was turning eerie.

The all adrenaline high octane heavy metal workout instrumental (played in her ear pods) soon began to ache the head, forcing to the stoppage of music.

Clueless, soon she sat down in middle of the road and her heart beats turned aberrant. The rhythm so erratic and the pump so heavy that Adrija was clearly able to hear her irregular thumps, in the all heavily pin-drop silence atmosphere.

Suddenly Adrija began to feel some reverberation striking her ear drums and something or someone approaching from behind. Uncanny being the situation, she refrained from turning back. Helpless, Adrija broke down and tears began to roll down her cheeks.

The winds, the bushy sound and the howling/cry of the animals from the backdrop- the entire setting had somewhat gripped

Adrija. It made her believe of the paranormal forces hovering around. Also, no one coming out to walk, further validated the feeling. Adrija continued to sit in middle of the road and wept nonstop with closed eyes. Unable to find anyone for help she began to chant God's name and prayed for some kind of intervention.

After a heavy forty-five minutes, finally there was a daybreak and the weather appeared to clear up. Suddenly from behind, Adrija felt a hand on her left shoulder. Terrified, she screamed her lungs out and threw away the hand with full power (trying to get rid of the same).

Adrija began yelling," Please help, oh Lord please help, somebody please help! HELLLLPPPPPPP....!!!" and continued to do so.

Looking at all the fuss, the man actually standing behind was unable to understand the reason behind Adrija's madness. He was unaware of what Adrija felt and found himself in a fix. After almost a minute of fright the man said, "Have you lost it? I am here to help and on the contrary you seem to scare me. Turn back and look at me, I am the forest officer. What is wrong with you, madam? Sitting in the middle of the road, do you wish to end our life? Get up, get aside and hop on the bike, I will drop you till the exit."

Adrija did not turn. She was dead scared and had no mettle to turn around. The man feared to touch her again, as he had already experienced Adrija not being comfortable with the same. However, he decided to give another try. He again kept his hand on the other shoulder of hers and said, "Madam, look back please."

Gathering all strength Adrija managed to look back and found the man truly standing. She continued to shiver, had gone pale out of fright but somehow accumulated courage and extended her hand to double check his presence. To her relief, the man's presence turned out to be a reality and being no possession or a ghost.

On confirming the same, Adrija took help of the forest officer to get up. She could not feel her feet and had gone numb. Somehow she did manage to get back to normalcy (rather she tried to get normal) and grasped some breath.

On finding Adrija in discomfort, officer asked, "Madam you alright? We have an emergency hospital in the jungle, if you feel uneasy I can take you there."

"No just drop me to the exit please and I shall be fine," replied Adrija still breathing heavy.

The forest officer got on his two-wheeler and turned on the engine. Adrija upon hearing the ignition, hopped on to the pillion and the two left. As they traveled through the jungle, Adrija kept her eyes closed, held the officer tight from around the waist and continued to chant Lord's name.

As they reached the exit gate, "Madam, you may open your eyes and get down. We have reached," said the forest officer.

Adrija got off the bike, "Thank you sir. You saved my life," saying this she bowed down and soon left afterwards.

Adrija quickly got back to the hostel and locked herself in to the room. She gained some breath and settled on her bed. She grabbed the water bottle kept on the side table (besides her bed), hurried she opened the lid and quenched the thirsty throat.

Adrija still got tremors and was unable to digest the episode. She was unable to gain control on her muscles and continued to quake.

Talking to self she said, "What I just witnessed was really spooky. The same is the result of what I have done in the past. It is coming to haunt me and wanting to take revenge. It has been years but these people are not leaving me alone. I am not going to win over this and surely the end is near. What do I do?" and she kept blabbering in a monotonous tone without catching any breath.

Confused and inept to figure out the exit from the tragic situation; she got up from the bed and began to search for something. Adrija peeped in to every possible space- under the bed, below the center table, in all the drawers like those of the side and study table, a small iron cupboard near the window and every possible corner but unsuccessful.

Finally, she turned to the wardrobe and it was the only hope left. Adrija was on a mission and not going to rest until she had what she wanted. On continuing the hunt, she started talking to self (again) and said, "Where the fuck I have kept it? I need to find the same. I need to put down my feelings and relax my soul a bit. Where the hell are you?"

Adrija removed all her clothes hung and unfolded every possible pleated cloth. Ultimately, in a yellow satin stole she came across something really hard. She undraped and to her respite, "Here you are veiling down under. Look at the mess you have led to," said Adrija talking to the unveiling object hiding underneath and simultaneously pointing at the entire room, which literally looked like some filthy street market.

And what came out from the fabric was a black colored diary with written over it – 'THE CONFESSION MEMOIRE'. Adrija hugged the diary tight and leaving the created mess aside, instantly got to the study table.

On positioning herself, Adrija kissed the cover of the diary, placed it on the table top and turned the pages. She kept turning pages and did so, till she could find a fresh blank page. Finally, on coming to one she began to write.

Adrija wrote and wrote and jotted for about an hour, non-stop. Her expressions changed in the process, whilst writing. She regained calmness and felt way better than before. On putting down (whatever she wanted to) her feelings on paper, Adrija ultimately heaved a sigh of relief.

As she closed her diary, Adrija said, "It is you, who has been my permanent mate ever since I started comprehending the world around me. Thank you for being there."

With this she kissed the cover of the diary yet again, hugged to the chest and appeared relaxed. Adrija got up from the table, draped the diary back (in the stole) but this time kept it at a place more easily accessible.

As she put the diary back to a new place, Adrija immediately went to the telephone lounge and dialed Rudra's number. She was lucky this time on not having Fatima around. As soon as Rudra picked up, Adrija said, "Rudra I want to spend my entire life with you. I am tired of staying alone. I am in my last term of this degree and it's ending in 3 months. Let's settle down after that. And for this, you need to meet my dad first."

Rudra was shocked on this sudden confession. Before this, neither had proposed officially nor Adrija ever mentioned that she was this fond of him. He had mixed feelings- on one side he felt delighted and felt like celebrating; on the other he did not know what to answer on this 'DAD' thing. He was not prepared for the same. Rudra appeared lost and went speechless. He could not react and had rather turned blank.

"Rudra you there? Can you hear me? You sure of getting married to me right? You very well knew I was not in for any casual affair. Rudra! Rudra?" Adrija panicked on not having any response from Rudra.

"I am right here, listening to you. And I myself went in to this relationship with an intent of being together forever. I am ready to meet anyone. It's just that we need to discuss this once face-to-face and plan the meeting with your dad," replied Rudra trying to calm Adrija down.

"Sure. Ok Fatima is coming. Just message me the next meeting as usual and I shall be there," with this Adrija kept the call and went back to her room.

After a week-

Adrija got to the telephone lounge and called up Rudra, "Hi. How are you? How have you been doing? I am waiting for you to plan a trip, but you seem to have not turn up after that dad conversation."

"I have been running busy and nothing came up in Mumbai. Also, I have been prohibited from calling or texting, so if I wish to talk, I am not allowed to," replied a helpless Rudra.

"Hmmmm… ok I am sorry. But guess what? I have called you for something really exciting," replied Adrija filled with enthusiasm.

Rudra could sense something nice coming his way and all curious he asked, "Please tell fast, I am waiting to hear the good news."

"Fatima is gone to her hometown due to an emergency, so it will not be that difficult to call you for next one week. But I wish to meet you in person and that too at the hostel," replied Adrija grinning.

"Are you kidding me? You want me to come down to your hostel? The GIRLS hostel? NO ways this could be true! You are trying to pull my legs," reacted Rudra out of disbelief.

"I have made friends with the security at the back gate and the room is just opposite to the same on the ground floor. So, you get it Mr. Rudra, I am not joking and very much serious of having you here next to me," said Adrija trying to convince Rudra.

"OMG. I am still not able to believe this and possibly won't, till I actually be besides you. How about me coming day after? It is a Sunday. You will be free from all the lectures and we will get more time to spend together," replied an elated Rudra.

"Done. Ok then see you," said Adrija.

"For sure. Very much dying to see you. Bye," responded Rudra in his cheeky best.

"Bye," and Adrija disconnected with a huge smile on hearing the typical Rudra kind of reply.

The next day passed by and both were equally thrilled to meet. Rudra left on Sunday early morning at 7 AM for Mumbai. While Adrija got off the bed and after doing her mundane morning stuff, took out the personal diary and sat.

Adrija was very happy, and maybe she wanted to pen down the same feeling in her book. As she wrote, she was not the same Adrija like before (the day she was on the day of forest incident) and with all serenity noted everything what she felt, taking her time. Pausing intermittently and not bothered about time, she smiled, she blushed and appeared pretty much relaxed while writing.

Suddenly, her phone rang. Picking up the phone she said, "Yes Bahadur ji."

"Madam ji, the guy has come and I am getting him inside. Keep the door open. Quick," replied Bahadur.

Hearing this Adrija freaked out. Her diary was right in front and the distance between the hostel gate and her room was less than 25 meters. She surely did not want her personal stuff to be seen by anybody and clueless she panicked. Quickly she kept the diary in the drawer of her side table and opened the door. As she opened, Rudra along with Bahadur, stood right in front.

Bahadur saluted Adrija and left. While Rudra on the other hand getting in, smiled and said, "What timing! It felt like those typical film-scenes where the heroine senses the incoming of her hero and without bell being rung the doors open and the couple smiles."

"Just shut-up and make yourself comfortable," reacted Adrjia on seeing Rudra getting under the skin of typical him.

Rudra sat on the chair next to study table and looked around at the room. And still wandering around he said, "I am sure your dad earns really good, the room is no less than the five-star hotel accommodation. It has everything and is pretty spacious."

Adrija gave a death stare. As Rudra termed her eyes came with a message, at the moment it did convey the same- mess at your own risk. Rudra understood and felt maintaining silence being the best option.

Adrija pulled another chair from the corner of the room and sat next to Rudra. Holding his hands, Adrija said, "Rudra I know I never made it official and never expressed of liking you. I also understand how you must have felt that day on me telling you of meeting my Dad all of a sudden. But I also know I was serious about the entire conversation that day and want us to settle down. I LOVE YOU RUDRA."

The expression immediately made Rudra emotional and his eyes turned moist. He had tears of joy and did not feel like stopping them from rolling down. The efforts had paid off and the conviction had turned true.

From the very first day, Rudra was adamant and stubborn of this getting converted in to something beautiful. Ideally, it was a dream coming true kind of a moment for Rudra. He was wordless and astounded.

Wiping his tears, Adrija continued smirking, "I know you have been wanting to hear this from long. I know it's a feeling difficult to seep in. But all thanks to your undying spirit and unruffled efforts, this has happened. C'mon speak something even I am waiting to hear the reply."

"I am Heaven-ified," reacted Rudra coming to his very character.

On hearing the reply, Adrija burst out laughing

"I love you to the infinity, beyond this universe and the stars in the galaxy. I wish to spend my entire life with you and promise to hold your hand till death gets us apart," continued Rudra with a tighter grip on the hands and full assurance.

With this Adrija got up, asked Rudra to do the same and she hugged. She hugged him really tight. The embracement was filled with warmth and such love, that the feelings in the individual's heart seemed like transferring, with no words needed.

Rudra could sense the growth in Adrija's confidence and belief with the squeeze, that she gradually developed during this journey. The two transported to another world and the feeling was nevertheless incredible.

The hug lasted for over 5 minutes and soon after they got back to their seats. They ordered food from outside, had fun chit-chatting and lived every bit spent together.

It had turned evening and the clock displayed 5 P. M. Suddenly, someone knocked the door. Adrija and Rudra both panicked and had turned clueless because of the suddenly developed situation. The two went blank as the knocking of the door continued.

Soon, Adrija heard, "Madam open the door it's me, Bahadur. Quickly madam." This gave some composure to the nervy situation and Adrija went on to open the door.

"Bahadur, you scared me. What happened? Why are you beating the door this hard," said an irritated Adrija.

"Sorry, Madam. But Dean is calling you and a few other final year students to her cabin. She wants to meet you all and convey something important," replied Bahadur in a soft tone.

"Ok. But is there anything to worry? And is it ok if I leave my friend here? Could you please keep a watch and make sure nobody comes to the room," requested Adrija as she turned apprehensive.

"Yes madam. Nothing to worry. Dean has called others too, so it must be something related to academics. I will take care of the situation. You please go and meet the dean," replied Bahadur assuring Rudra's safety.

"Thank you, Bahadur," with this she gestured Rudra of coming back in a while and he replied with a thumbs-up signal.

Bahadur on the other hand, "Saab let me know if you need anything or if anything bothers you. I am right at the gate," said Bahadur and left providing his phone number.

Rudra was all alone and on his own, which is when came an idea of exploring every inch of the room. He got up from the chair and started with the wardrobe. On seeing the clothes hung that Adrija had worn on dates (when the two met), he smiled and recollected every bit of the moment spent together. All those meetings came in front of him like a flashback and he could not believe that it had come down to this (today where Adrija actually expressed her love for him). He casually checked the drawers and every possible space of the wardrobe. He then turned to the iron cupboard, the drawers of the tables and finally to the side table near the bed.

On opening the drawer, he saw that black diary of Adrija and murmured, *"THE CONFESSION MEMOIRE.* Sounds interesting. It must be her personal diary and would help me know more about her. It would provide an insight of her life experiences and help me understand her better."

Saying this he kept the diary in his bag that he got along and went to the window. The outside of the window had beautiful garden-area view with different color flowers enhancing the landscape. Rudra continued to peek outside the window for some time. Not realizing the time passed by, Rudra was immersed in some thought of his own and forgotten about Adrija's absence. After thirty minutes, Adrija arrived and immediately hugged Rudra from behind.

"Is everything alright?" asked Rudra as he turned to the front and continued to provide warmth.

"Yes, just the usual academics motivation and her expectations of topping the university. I just wanted to feel you so ya," replied Adrija as she continued to squeeze him tight. The two appeared inseparable and was the purest of the feelings.

Soon, Adrija got to the bed of hers and said, "Now we need to plan a meet with my dad. We need to convince him and settle down." To this Rudra nodded without any hesitation.

"And when & how we do that?" asked Rudra.

"I think he will be coming down to Mumbai next month so we can plan the same. You still got about 30 days or more to prepare for the encounter," said Adrija.

She pulled Rudra through his shirt, got him really close to her face and continued, "You better make sure he is influenced by your charm or else wait and watch," and she kissed his cheeks.

Rudra was immovable and had been hypnotized. He was seeing Adrija this close for the very first time and appeared spellbound as he looked in her blue-eyes. The kiss was like an icing on the cake. He so wanted to return the love in the form she did, but feared of appearing like going over-board. Hence, he decided to just go with the flow.

As the two went on to share the cozy moments and the clock went past 7 P. M, Adrija said, "I think you should leave before it gets too late and someone comes at the door."

"I do not want this day to get over and so wish the time freezes right here, at this moment. I want to capture this moment and store it in my heart forever. I so want to be with you, but yes will have to leave" replied Rudra with a heavy heart.

On hearing this Adrija got up and hugged Rudra again. She kissed both his cheeks with impact and said, "We will meet soon. These good-byes are the one that give you a hope of meeting again."

Rudra could not resist this time and returned the favor, kissing on one of her cheeks. She shied and went red blushing. Rudra went stress-free on seeing the positive reaction.

"Take care and see you really soon," with this he bid bye and left on a happy note.

Leaving the hostel, he went on to find a hotel in Mumbai as Rudra had a meeting on the following day. On checking in, there was a thought that continuously troubled his mind. The thought of getting the personal diary without informing Adrija. Although, his intent was pure and wanted to know more about her, but it made Rudra feel heavy inside.

The discomfort continued to bother him, especially after the faith that Adrija showed today and the way they came closer. But now that it was done, there was no returning back.

CHAPTER 4
THE BOOK MYSTERY

On convincing himself on the diary part, Rudra went to the hotel's restaurant for dinner. He removed his phone and kept looking on the past photographs of his and Adrija's togetherness. Rudra smiled on every memory recollected and it widened with every pic swiped.

Suddenly, the conversation of Adrija asking him to meet her dad struck his mind. The very thought of meeting Adrija's dad had made Rudra conscious and uneasy. He was sure of taking this relationship forward and wished to settle down with her, but the very thought of meeting somebody's parent (that he had never ever done before) had made him go numb.

Rudra soon finished dinner and walked nonstop in the hotel lounge. He so wanted to meet someone with whom Rudra could share his feelings at the moment. But the problem was, Rudra had lost touch with all his past contacts and knew nobody in Mumbai, except Adrija.

On seeing him walk continuously and with restlessness, one of the waiters came and asked, "Was the food alright sir? Is there anything that is causing a problem? May I help you?"

"No no I am fine. I think I have over-eaten. The food was so sumptuous that I could not control, hence the stride," and with this Rudra left for the room.

On returning back to the room, he continued to gait. After a brisk walk of about 30 minutes, Rudra could recollect of his old time school-friend Aazad Khan staying in Mumbai. Six months back, he had accidentally met him on one of the occasions at the local railway station, and was also invited by Aazad to visit his apartment then.

Aazad had studied along with Rudra in school and the two were best of friends, then. Later, they chose different career options and the connection weakened but the momentum was maintained as they caught up occasionally like once or twice every month. But this was when the two stayed in Pune.

It had been long now (almost 4 years, the time since the two started earning) the two had lost touch and only communicated over call. That too came to a halt since Adrija entered in Rudra's life.

Rudra felt awkward connecting with Aazad and that too out of work, but had no choice. He desperately wanted to calm his anxiety and settle the butterflies in the stomach. So keeping all the discomfort aside, he blatantly dialed up and, "Hi Aazad how are you? Rudra this side."

"Hey buddy good to hear you. I am doing great, how about you?" replied Aazad from the other side of the phone.

"Nothing great, just the usual life. I was in Mumbai so thought of catching up over a coffee or lunch tomorrow?" replied Rudra.

"Lunch sounds difficult as I have a meeting scheduled in the second half right after the lunch break. We can meet over coffee post 4.30 P. M," replied Aazad

"Hey hold on. I stay alone and the society is really peaceful. You can turn up at my place rather than meeting outside. We can chill, relax, talk peacefully and have a nice reunion. If it sounds okay to you," came a casual invitation from Aazad.

Rudra was more than happy and could not control his excitement. Instantly he said, "Ok then meet you at 4.30 p.m," and accepted the invitation.

As much as the day spent (with Adrija) felt beautiful and appeared short-lived; the night on the other hand appeared lengthy and tough to get through.

Two thoughts continuously drummed in his cerebrum and created stir- one the diary thing; second the meeting part. He was finding it difficult to overcome the pondering thoughts and fall asleep. Somehow, the night passed Rudra finished his assignment the next morning (for which he had come down to Mumbai) and post lunch he just waited to meet Aazad.

Finally, it was time and Rudra went on to meet Aazad.

At Aazad's residence-

Rudra stood outside Aazad's house and pressed the door-bell. Aazad on opening the door, "Hey buddy it has been really long. Please come in," saying this Aazad hugged Rudra and invited him in.

As Rudra stepped in, he said, "Really long. Even our last encounter was at the railway station and that too only for a couple of minutes."

"Yes I remember. Even that seems like ages. Please sit and make yourself comfortable," said Aazad as he gestured towards the couch and asked Rudra to take seat.

Rudra on sitting down, looked around and spoke nothing. The nervousness was clearly evident on his face and on getting noticed, "You seem to be here for something that is bothering you inside. You are still the same. You cannot hide the tension and your facial expression conveys it all. I am still the same Aazad and here to help you. You need not wait for any formal talks and can begin. Its ok! Shoot!," said Aazad.

Rudra once again felt awkward to begin the conversation with the stress that troubled him; but he wanted to get off those apprehensions. Yet again barefacedly he began, "I love a girl and madly so. This has been going around for a couple of months now. She just suddenly proposed like yesterday, to settle down with her forever, which is fine. But she threw a situation at me, which has got me in a fix."

"And the situation being?" asked Aazad.

"She wants me to meet her dad," came a prompt reply from Rudra.

Aazad laughed out loud and felt Rudra's reply being really stupid. Also, as per Aazad this was no big of a problem, it was just another meet with a stranger which sooner or later is going to be a part of the family.

However, on seeing Rudra getting irritated, he stopped chuckling and, "What big deal? Obviously, you got to meet her parents for the same. Even she would be meeting your parents someday right? So what is it that has got you to this nervy kind of a thing?" asked Aazad in a casual tone.

"I don't know. I am not prepared yet. I have a few work related assignments coming up. They are really big and important. Also, I do not wish to induce my energies in convincing her dad or anything for that matter and only aim to give my 100 percent to the upcoming projects," replied Rudra hesitantly.

"Buddy you cannot do away with this and got to face the same," replied Aazad making him realize that this meeting being equally important. Although, it sounded like a tough task but had to be prioritized.

To this Rudra nodded superficially and continued, "This is not it. There is one more thing that is bothering me since last night." With this Rudra opened the bag (he carried along) and removed Adrija's diary.

"What is this? A Book? This is bothering you?" asked Aazad as he grinned looking at the book.

"This is not any book. It is Adrija's personal diary," replied Rudra.

"WHAT! THE CONFESSION MEMOIRE," said Aazad as he snatched the book from Rudra's hand.

"You got to be kidding Rudra. You stole the book? You love the person madly and you did not have the balls to ask her upfront about the past? You are such a doubtful of a nature, that to dig her past relationships and to study about her EX's, you just got the book hiding from the lady you love. Impossible that you love her. This is not any kind of love at all," a pissed Aazad reprimanded.

"I have no doubts, nor do I care about her past. I don't know what happened that day and I just carried the book along. I thought of confessing to Adrija about the same but, the instants that took shape on the very day, held me back with a fear of things going out of control. I just wanted to understand her and which is why I did what I did," replied Rudra justifying his deed.

"This is impossible. You are not even ready to accept the mistake. Then what kind of guilt is inside that has got you here?" asked Aazad as he appeared annoyed.

"The guilt has not got me here. The anxiety of meeting her dad is the reason why I am standing right in front of you. I thought of sharing my apprehensions with my best friend. Also, I did not read the book alone because I felt- if I get stuck somewhere and unable to find a solution myself, then it will be my best friend who will sail me through this," replied Rudra in a sulking tone.

Aazad eased a little and his strut appeared to relax a bit. He got out of the distress zone and realized the duty of helping his buddy. "Okay then let's go ahead with the diary first. This will give me an insight about Adrija's life and help me to help you on meeting her dad and other things," said Aazad in a mild tenor.

"Great. Get going," said Rudra gesturing Aazad to start reading the diary.

"What do I do?" asked a confused Aazad.

"Open and read," replied Rudra in a casual tone.

"Seriously! You want me to read aloud your GF's personal diary?" asked Aazad.

"Yes. I cannot. I don't know I am unable to open it. So go ahead and start. Quick," replied Rudra.

"Unbelieveable man. First you get the diary and then you are unable to read. Moreover, you ask me to read your girlfriend's personal stuff. What kind of a person are you? Unbelieveable man!" said Aazad in disappointment.

On hearing the same Rudra gave a riled glare, ignoring which Aazad held the diary, took a deep breath and began reading, "So this is the first chapter of the book that says- **THE NIGHT I WILL NEVER FORGET.**"

"Ok. This sounds really emotional. With the kind of title to the chapter, it seems to be a sensitive one. Go on and read the body," replied Rudra.

Aazad avoided the inputs given by Rudra and began reading-

"The day that final match took place on 2nd April, 2011- every Indian celebrated the triumph of the team. But for me it was an unforgettable nightmare. My mom didn't know that I was looking from behind the pillar. The entire episode quaked me from inside. I curse myself for getting up at the wrong time (as I felt hungry) and witnessing what I witnessed. My dad and also my hero, took his last breath right in front of my eyes. I could not believe it was my mom who KILLED him. Like his initials of the name, he used to crack silly jokes but still we used to laugh. And laugh like no one saw us. Yes, PJ (Piyush Jha) was killed by my mom. She hit the liquor bottle on my father's head and broke it. The impact was such that it led to excessive bleeding and the same was irrepressible. Thus, causing an instant death of my BFF- PJ," read the first page of the diary.

"Hold on. Are you sure this is what the first chapter of the diary reads? Are you kidding? She said like just yesterday, that its time that we meet her father. However, here the story appears altogether different. Like even I told you that I am nervous to meet her dad and which is why I am here. But, this article in the memoir, exhibits a different angle to the story" asked Rudra out of perplexity.

"I am not good at making stories this quick. I am not any filmmaker nor this is my personal memoir. Even I am shocked to read what is written and was coming to ask you that- is this some kind of a joke? On the contrary you seem to be asking me my question," replied Aazad.

"I can't believe it. I don't know whom to trust. I mean I am sure nobody lies in the personal diary, but she talking about her dad and that too so casually and this frequently is worrisome. What I believed to be an emotional chapter before the start, now frightens me," said Rudra as he sweated in an all air-conditioned room. The thought of his dad being already dead years back, gave him chills.

Aazad turned the page and continued, "After she murdered my dad, she did apologize and realized that what she did was wrong; but it was too late. And the body (of PJ that lied in the pool of blood) could neither punish nor forgive my mom. Well, my mother doesn't know that I know and I have decided to not tell her the same. I want her to face him and apologize for what she did. THE END," read the second page and the chapter ended right there.

"Hold on I am feeling dizzy and my head is revolving. I am unable to understand the mindset of the little girl writing this. Formerly, she mentioned her mother apologizing to the very body and in the latter half she writes the mother needs to say sorry upfront. What does this indicate?" a bamboozled Rudra said, unable to get hold of things and understand what they actually meant.

"GOD! I never thought the one whom I would love, will be full of mystery and enigma. I am heading somewhere directionless and I don't know whom to reach out for help," Rudra further continued.

"Stop being over-dramatic Rudra. You are acting naïve. Just tell me one thing- did she ever mention about her mother? Anything that you can recollect or share or help with?" asked Aazad.

"Oh yes! I forgot to share this. Adrija once said, that her parents had separated, post which she continued to live with her dad. So I never bothered to ask any further," replied Rudra with some respite.

"Damn! Now this is inconclusive. The statement doesn't match with the theory mentioned in the diary. Is it possible that she likes writing and must have weaved a story? You know the fiction drama types. I mean she must have thought of giving a different angle to the World Cup night saga. Possible right?" asked Aazad.

"I cannot confirm on anything. I have never heard of Adrija being a passionate or professional writer. Nor did I ever come across any situation that indicates of her being creative in prose," replied Rudra with no improvement in his condition.

"Then what I see this as, is something that has hidden between the lines and needs a broader prospect to understand, "replied Aazad, feeling miserable.

"So now what? How do we find out the truth? How do we know is this a fantasy story or reality? How would we know her father is dead or alive? What will be the next step? I love Adrija and cannot leave her on the mere basis of the very fact that she hallucinates her dead father's presence (if the story in the diary turns out to be true). I want a solution and getting apart won't be the one for sure. This would damage her emotionally and mentally, rather than healing her," replied a concerned Rudra, deeply soaked in Adrija's love.

"Stop right there. You are going over-board and throwing permutations to the story. There could be anything. Why can't we think on her creative part and be positive?" shouted Aazad on seeing Rudra over-react.

"Because the chances of the positive side of the story are minute. I have seen her going in that zone and talking unrealistic things. She has told me few times sub-consciously, things that has been repeated from her past or few moments where she felt uncomfortable, but I felt those were out of stress. But now it feels like those blabber chats made sense," replied Rudra as he felt low on confidence.

"Well then, there can be only one person who can help us out of this. I know this Dr. Krisha Menon. She is a renowned psychiatrist, hand-writing analyst and a close friend of mine," said Aazad assuming this being the only ray of hope in the dark.

"Psychiatrist? How would we convince Adrija?" asked Rudra on hearing the Doctor's name out of the blue.

"Why would you want to take Adrija to Dr. Menon?" asked a bamboozled Aazad.

"You just said we need to visit your friend. So what does that mean?" asked Rudra further getting jumbled up.

"OMG. You are ridiculous and incorrigible. Man, what I meant is, we will take the diary along and show it to my friend. She will analyse the same and help us understand Adrija's mindset. Did you get it or should I give a detailed description?" said a frustrated Aazad.

Rudra nodded and could not believe the heights of his dumbness. Ignoring further discussion on the diary stuff, the concentration shifted to some-thing else very soon. "Close-friend! Hmmmmm… How close? Girl-friend? Mushy-mushy, hush-hush," said Rudra teasing Aazad.

"Shut up. She is just a friend. Also, let me tell you Krisha recently got married. We studied together in junior college and still very much in touch. That's the only story nothing more, nothing less," replied Aazad upfront with a poker face.

"Ok. My all condolences to you," came a quick reply from Rudra.

"Condolences? She's alive," came a prompt reply from Aazad.

"Oh yes, she very much is. I know. But I can feel the pain when you expressed of Krisha recently tying the knot with someone else. You had feelings for sure and I am offering sympathies for those departed feelings. Got it my failed lover," replied Rudra patting on Aazad's back. Aazad realized, appreciated Rudra's understanding and kept mum.

Almost after a minute of a silence, Rudra said, "So when can we meet her? By the way- What a co-incidence! I am here wanting to help my love and you associating with Krisha for this, sounds destiny. This in a way, will even allow you to spend some time with her."

"I want my feelings to heal and you are trying to sprinkle salt on my wounds," replied Aazad out of dismay.

"Well that is your POV (point of view). Look at it from my perspective- it will get you close to your love and make you feel better. Maybe this will give a closure to your one sided love and help you move on," replied Rudra infusing hope and optimism in Aazad.

To this Aazad nodded. The very thought of meeting Krisha brightened his face.

"Why don't we continue reading the diary further? Let us know what all she has gone through or be aware of her experiences," said Rudra with all curio and eagerness to know what's next.

"Well I suggest we continue further reading after meeting Krisha. You are already recovering from a shocker and I don't think you are in any mood to take any more blows below the belt," replied Aazad trying to calm Rudra's nerves.

Rudra gazed at Aazad with raised eyebrows and agreed to his request with heavy heart. Just before Rudra could poke further, Aazad took the phone kept on charge on the table and dialed Krisha's number.

The phone rang and as soon as Krisha answered the call, Aazad put the phone on loudspeaker and said, "Hi Krisha. How you doing?"

To this Krisha on the other side of the phone replied, "Hey Aazad where have you been? You didn't even make it to my wedding. Is everything alright? I was worried for you, but just that the adjustments in the new atmosphere did not allow me to ask about your well-being. Anyways, good you called up. Tell me how are you? I am doing great."

"She doesn't even breathe while speaking. Is she always this talkative?" murmured Rudra giving a stare to Aazad.

"Just shut the fuck up. You are on loudspeaker. It will be a problem if she listens. Just be quiet," an angry Aazad responded.

"Hello, Aazad are you there? Whom are you talking to? I can hear something at the background? Is everything fine?" asked an anxious Krisha.

"Yes, yes. All good. Actually TV was on and so you could hear the noise in the background. I have muted the same. Tell me. So where was I?" replied Aazad gasping some breath and signaling Rudra to not speak anything any further.

"I asked how are you? I haven't heard form you since long," Krisha repeated her question.

"Yes I am all good. Actually, Krisha I wanted to talk to you about a case. I want an appointment, so that I can further share details and discuss it in person. If you don't mind, could you provide with the earliest appointment?" said Aazad, coming straight to the point.

"Ouch! Aazad that was really bang on and to the point. You called me out of work? I can't believe you being this mean. I thought you called me for a casual conversation," replied a disappointed Krisha.

Aazad banged the head (hitting the palm on the forehead) and pretending said, "I do want to talk to you, but I thought meeting in person and having a chat over a cup of coffee will be more pleasing. Isn't it?"

"Sho-sweet. Surely. Cool then let's meet at my office tomorrow 2 pm," replied an excited Krisha in all coy tone.

"Just one more thing Krisha, I will be getting a friend of mine along. Actually it is him who wants to meet you and talk about her fiancé," said Aazad.

"Ok. Get him along. See you guys tomorrow at 2 pm," replied Krisha and disconnected the call.

"What is this? What is wrong with you my boy? Good you did not get along with her for a lifetime. She is insane and too much over the top. You would not have been able to handle her after a while, I bet," said Rudra as Aazad kept the call.

"Oh yes! She possibly might be little nuts but yours is totally unpredictable. You still love her right?" replied Aazad turning emotional.

And it hit the soul hard, really hard. Rudra felt the prick right in the center and understood well, of not making fun of someone's love or nature.

Leaving the personal discrepancies aside and forgetting about the incidents that took place in last hour or so; the two continued that evening sharing the past experiences, recalling the old school memories and everything that added to the fun. The conversation continued till late and time just flew.

CHAPTER 5

THE MENON ANALYSIS

Next day being a Sunday, Rudra decided to stay back at Aazad's residence. The two got up really late around 1pm and rushed on the things (regular mundane) soon after. Rudra did not want to be late because he wanted the mystery to unfold; while Aazad had his reasons of meeting his love (again after really long) and hence hurried.

All dressed up and raring to go, Rudra and Aazad left. They reached the clinic. Upon seeing Aazad, Krisha was more than happy and said, "Hey how have you been. So good to see you." And she hugged him tight. Mind you it was nowhere close to a friendly hug, but way beyond.

Aazad on receiving the warmth looked surprised, but after a few seconds of shyness, he too responded with equal affection. While, Rudra on seeing the two exchanging the cordiality, felt mystified and wondered what was going on. The lady just married another guy and here she doesn't appear to leave Aazad at all. He just stood beside and saw the drama unfolding of the two lost love-birds.

Finally, Krisha left Aazad and said, "You smell really good. I like it."

Rudra was confounded further as she sniffed and gave a wretched look to Aazad. Aazad noticed the same and felt mortified. He knew how Rudra had the habit of drawing conclusions and was aware of something really senseless coming from Rudra (as he continued to give vile stare).

"Hey Hi. And you are?" asked Krisha finally able to see there was one more person along with Aazad.

"I am Rudra. I thought I would be out of focus throughout this meet. But I am lucky to get noticed by you," replied Rudra in all sarcasm.

Krisha gave a fake smile to the reply and invited the two in. She received a call on her cell phone, seeing which she said, "You guys please make yourself comfortable. I got to answer this one and shall be back soon," and she walked out of her cabin.

As soon as Rudra seated on the chair, "Are you sure she did not have feelings for you? She willingly got married to the guy or was she forced by the family? Trust me she too has a soft corner and very much deeply in love with you," he murmured in the ears of Aazad.

"Just shut up and don't create a mess. It was a usual hug and nothing more," replied an irritated Aazad.

"Usual hug? It was just day before yesterday that I received such a hug from Adrija. After dating for more than a quarter of a year, I got an opportunity of hugging her, this casually. And you are saying it was a plain hug," said Rudra with all doubts and suspicion.

"She was getting inside your shirt and smelling the cologne. If this would have lasted for a few more seconds, then she would have even sensed the smell of the body wash that you use for bathing. Just don't give me that friendly wala vibe. It was nowhere near to that," said Rudra in all satirical tone.

Aazad was about to reply. But just before he could open his mouth, the cabin door opened and Krisha upon entering said, "Sorry to keep you guys waiting. Tell me how can I help you?"

"Now who is coming straight to the point? You felt so when I did the same on call yesterday, right? I thought we were here for a coffee first and then would talk about the official work," replied Aazad on not missing an opportunity to give Krisha a taste of her own medicine.

Seeing the same, Krisha said, "I get flattered all the time, when you talk to me like that. You never hide what you feel and are upfront always."

"Let us have coffee first and then for sure discuss the matter," saying this she picked up the receiver and, "Kadam, get three cup of coffee, quick."

Rudra's eyeballs widened on seeing the two getting mushy-mushy. Also, he felt Krisha was appearing too coy for no reason. As the thoughts did march-past in Rudra's mind, the coffee arrived.

Kadam placed the cups right in front and asked Aazad, "Sugar for you sir?"

Krisha immediately intervened," Sugarless for him, he likes it strong," and gave a kinky smile to Aazad.

Kadam appeared shell-shocked and so did Rudra on seeing Krisha respond on behalf of Aazad. "It's ok, just add half a spoon to my cup and stop being stupefied. This has been going on since we have come here," said Rudra gesturing Kadam to close his dropped jaw.

Kadam soon served the coffee to all and left. Krisha gave a death stare to Rudra, to which he obviously avoided and concentrated on his cappuccino. Aazad felt uncomfortable amidst all this, but had no option and continued to feel awkward.

As the three finished coffee, Rudra said, "Can we now get down to business? Or shall we wait for some cookies next?"

On hearing upon, Aazad stamped on Rudra's foot, indicating him to be sensible and if he cannot, then better to keep the mouth shut. To this Rudra reacted really loud and said, "Ouch! That hurt."

Krisha got a hint about the cat fight going on between the two boys and interjected, "Please ignore him Aazad and let him be the way he likes. And you young man, tell me what problem do you have? I mean why are we here for a session?"

Finally, Rudra had a relief on his face and without much of a delay, took out the book from his bag. "This is my girlfriend's personal diary and I want you to tell me about her state of mind by reading it," said Rudra as he placed the Memoir on the table.

"State of mind as in? Is she intellectually weak? Does she have some kind of a problem?" asked Krisha.

"That is why we are here. We want to know the perceptive behind her thinking and seeking for some answers, which we feel only you can guide us through," said Aazad in a soft-tone.

Krisha blushed hearing this and said, "Okay," as she took the diary in her hands.

Immediately after having the diary, she began to feel it by moving her hands on the texture of the book. She looked back and forth, not once but twice and said, "By the feel of the outer surface I can very well say that this is her personal diary and there are deep dark secrets hidden inside. Get ready to witness the unfolding of the world full of revelations and blows."

Aazad and Rudra looked at each other. Both were stunned on finding Krisha to be correct to the point; that too, without giving her any hint of what they read yesterday. Rudra, especially was shell-shocked on finding Krisha hit the bull's eye just by having her hands on the texture of the book.

The boys turned and looked at each other. They glared, stared and exchanged dialogues through their eyes. While they continued to do so, a common cryptic thought ran through the mind of both the boys out there - the theory of this being a fantasy write-up has been ruled out. So the only story that made sense was -her father being dead and her mother being the killer. This raised the anxiety levels and further left them fretful.

After an absolute silence of about 5 minutes, Rudra accumulated some guts and asked, "How can you be so sure?"

"Look at the cover, it is absolute plain black and nothing else on it. Also, if you see at the name of the book it says the confession memoir. This states there are things mentioned which she has failed to discuss with anyone or did not feel like sharing with anybody. So all these things make me conclude about the book," replied Krisha with unflustered confidence.

To this both the boys nodded as they were left with no other option and gestured Krisha to continue.

"So let us begin with the first chapter," saying this she began reading. Soon, she completed that section of the book and upon completion said, "What the hell? Her mother killed her husband? She must have gone through a lot after witnessing that horrifying episode. She was madly in love with her dad and I am sure Adrija would continue to do so for rest of her life."

"Are you sure she killed her? Is there a possibility of this being some fictional story where the writer wants to create an out of the box impact of that historic (World-Cup) night?" asked Aazad out of pseudo hopes.

"Of course not. She has penned her heart out and the sentiments are felt clearly. I feel for the little girl writing this. And what at a mere age of 10-12!" replied a confident Dr. Krisha.

"Forget it. Please continue on to the next chapter doctor," said Rudra on gulping the fact that her girlfriend hallucinated on her father's presence.

"Certainly. Chapter two- **Heart-broke on the debut**," read Krisha.

On hearing the title, the two wanted to believe this being a chapter of rejected love but chose otherwise and decided of not being judgmental. The first episode had something and meant something. So they rather prepared their minds for another jolt.

Accumulating guts Rudra said, "Please go ahead and read."

With this Krisha began to read, *"I was all set to experience the most wonderful feeling ever, but he left me dejected. I cannot believe and at this moment my every sense seems to have gone numb. After raising my expectations to sky high, Anand Kumar left me with a sensation of no more than hollow and void. I so wish I could take revenge and show him how it feels, but this being not the right time I am helpless. Nevertheless, I shall wait for MY TIME. THE END,"* and with this the second section ended.

On coming across this 'the end' stuff repetitively at the end of this chapter, similar to that of the previous one, Rudra felt something unusual. Unable to hold on the butterflies, "What is this 'THE END' theory at the finish of every section. What does that indicate doctor?" asked Rudra with all speculation.

"This shows that she is done with the emotion and would never return. She will never think of this part of her life, ever again. It is like she deletes the memory of what has hurt her but still keeps the incident locked, somewhere in one of the corners of her brain. The same can be retrieved when needed," replied Krisha with all her psychological expertise.

"Could you please translate the said part in to the layman's language!" said Aazad as everything seemed to have passed over the head.

"In simple words it is like formatting your phone or your hard disk getting crashed. Still able to retrieve the data from the same as and when required. Similarly, what I mean here is, she has a cold heart and does not crib if things are not going her way. But, she also keeps the stir alive and takes revenge when time permits," replied Krisha.

"Did I just hear the word revenge? What kind of revenge? What does she do? I mean such a heavy word oozes sweat from every pore on my body and makes me feel jittery. Could you please be clear on the revenge part, asap?" instantly asked Aazad who was literally seen sweating as he claimed.

"I will have to dig deep to understand the character of the person. For which I will also have to go through all the filled pages of the diary. This will help me to get under the skin of her character and give a better understanding about her psyche. So what I request you guys is to give me some time but be assured to treat this as a case of priority."

"Okay," and this left Aazad incomplete and dissatisfied with the reply.

Rudra was stumped on seeing Aazad this displeased and felt on him getting too emotionally attached to all this. Just before Aazad could add more displeasure to the situation, Rudra said, "Just one thing doctor- I love this girl beyond any available resource on this earth and would not want to leave her just because she has a psychological imbalance. I am sure of the fact that she is ill, but also confident of her being surely recoverable. So find a solution. PLEASE"

Krisha was awestruck. She appeared entranced on seeing his love for Adrija. Krisha could sense every beat of Rudra, having Adrija's name etched- bold and clear. The intent of being madly in love with her was visible. She constantly glared at Rudra and after a magnetic minute said, "Aaaaawwwwwww.... Adrija is so lucky to have you. I wish I had such an obsessed lover in my life who would have treated me in the same way- madly and unconditionally."

On hearing the reply, Rudra immediately murmured in Aazad's ear, "She doesn't know you are the same passionate lover. I wonder how she could read my eyes and surprisingly failed to do the same with yours. Good you did not get along with her."

"Shut your mouth and don't create an awkward moment," gave back Aazad.

On seeing the two whispering, Krisha said, "You can share the private talk with me boys. I will be more than happy to clear your doubts."

"I am sure you would be. Nothing important. Rudra just appears impatient and want to get out of this at the earliest. That's it," replied Aazad. Rudra gave a disinterested look and Krisha once again ignored the same.

"Ok so we shall take a leave and wait for your call?" said Aazad pointing towards the book.

"Oh yes absolutely. I will confront, once I am done with the reading," replied Krisha.

The two got up from their respective seats and shook hands with Krisha. As they reached the exit, "Looking forward to many more coffee's together, MINUS YOUR FRIEND. See you and take care," shouted Krisha from her seat and was finally seen hurling out all that was filled inside against Rudra.

Aazad looked back amazed and with a soft smile left, while Rudra gave a wicked look and took the exit.

As the two continued to walk out of the building, Rudra said, "Man she is totally unpredictable. She wants to have more coffees with you and that too leaving the man all alone to whom she recently got wed. This is unfair on the man and I really pity him."

"Stop over-acting, you third class actor. I know you felt envious because she literally ignored you in the end, which you even deserved, all thanks to your antics. I can smell the fire of jealousy" said Aazad.

Rudra felt stupid of what Aazad thought and considered silence being the best at that moment. From there on, the two left to their respective destinations.

A WEEK AFTER THE LAST MEET-

The next Sunday morning, around 10 A. M, Krisha called Aazad and over the call said, "Hi. How have you been?"

"Hey. I have been doing good. What about you? You called up this early on Sunday morning? Is everything alright?" asked Aazad in a concerned tone.

"All has been good but not that great. I just completed reading that book of your friend and….," Krisha took a sudden pause while speaking.

"Forget!" said Krisha in a heavy dejected tone.

She continued in a wobbling tone, "Can you get that friend of yours along, today at same time around 2 P. M?" The tone in which she invited did not brush on any positive vibes and rather indicated some sort of caution.

Aazad got the hint from the manner in which she spoke, and it already had his blood pressure elevated. Doubting the intent behind the urgency, Aazad asked, "What is it about? Is there anything from the personal diary? You can tell me. C'mon Krisha."

"Could you please come down to my office with no more questions asked? Is it possible today?" replied Krisha.

"Well yes, but what's the matter? You can tell me. It will be easier for me to convince Rudra in getting along. You know how he is! My ears will start resonating with his senseless questions, if I ask him for the visit without a proper explaination," replied Aazad pleading.

"I want you both here is all I want to say and get him anyhow. I will be waiting. Bye," with this Krisha disconnected the call.

Aazad was left high and dry. Without any second thoughts he called up Rudra and said, "Hi. Krisha just called up and have asked to see her at 2 P. M."

"Did she speak of anything else?" asked Rudra in a casual tenor.

"NO! She called to invite and did not talk anything beyond. So see you directly at the venue. Wait downstairs if you reach before me and vice-versa. We shall walk up together," replied Aazad in a best possible manner to dodge any further queries from Rudra.

"Okay," and Rudra disconnected.

The plain acceptance by Rudra, had Aazad wondering. Aazad expected Rudra to feel curious and wanted to throw questions at him. On the contrary a plain okay had further added to Aazad's discomfort. He could not digest the casual attitude of his friend. Where Krisha's call had made Aazad nervous, his call to Rudra had him unaffected. Aazad felt the uneasiness and continued to behave restless till he reached Krisha's office building at the given time.

Rudra upon reaching, observed Aazad in some sort of tension and with concern asked, "Is everything alright?"

Aazad saw Rudra being fine and relaxed, hence pretending to act normal replied, "Yes of course. Is there anything that made you ask me this?"

"I thought there is something that's bothering you. Your body language indicated so. Well I might be wrong. Let it go. Let's walk up?" asked Rudra.

"Sure," replied Aazad in a firm tenor.

The two reached the floor. On entering the cabin Rudra observed Krisha being not her usual self. She sat on her chair in despair and there were no welcome wishes either. The two seated and even before Rudra could utter, Aazad started, "I have been living in suspense for the past 4 hours and want to know what it is. The silence is causing me nervousness and I am unable to put hold on my emotions. Please speak."

To this Krisha reacted, "Well I read her entire diary boys," and with this she got up from the chair.

"And what did you find?" interjected Aazad.

Rudra on the other hand was calm and appeared composed. He

was prepared for any and everything. He had come with only one intent- to find a solution to the problem. Nothing more, nothing less. Seeing Aazad over-react he said, "Hold on man. You are off to a flier. Don't jump to conclusion so soon. She is going to disclose. Just keep your calm and relax a bit."

"So the diary is filled with full of dull moments (of her life), until you (pointing at Rudra) came in her life. The initial fifty odd pages just talk about the misfortunes, heartbreaks and tragedies that she has gone through, right from her childhood. And it is only after Rudra entering her life, that she revived and started living again," said Krisha in a sulking tone.

The last sentence that Krisha told, struck the chord right at the center of Rudra's heart and out of extreme happiness he got up and hugged the doctor. Out of goodness he said, "Thank you doctor. I knew she loves me really deep and you just attested the same by stating what you stated in the end. Thank you. Thank you. Thank you," and he continued to hug the doctor.

Krisha was shocked with this kind of reaction and more than her, the one who appeared traumatized was Aazad. Aazad could not see his friend hug his girlfriend (though one sided love) and felt resentful. Aazad got off the chair annoyed and separating Rudra said, "How can you pounce on her like an animal? She is a stranger to you and should think before doing what you did."

To this Krisha immediately replied, "It is okay Aazad, just relax. He did so, with harmless intention. It is absolutely fine."

"No it is not. He did so without your consent, which is wrong and totally unacceptable," said Aazad continuing to hyper-react.

"Hello. Stop defending which does not hold any importance. And where did this rebel inside you go, when she was getting married to someone else? That time you did not have balls to speak and now you are dancing like a monkey at a mere hug! Silly animal! Come on grow up Aazad. You should have expressed and not waited this long to come down to all this," said Rudra out of anguish and frustration.

"Just shut-up and stop ejecting shit out of your mouth. We are not here to analyze my mental peace," replied Aazad going red in the face. And the two kept quiet.

"Wait a minute. What do you mean by that Aazad? Rudra what is it that made you say all this. Why there is silence in the air all of a sudden? Will you boys tell me? Will the two of you tell me?" and she yelled out of ire. She approached Rudra and said, "Finish what has been started or I shall not tell what the diary speaks."

Rudra looked at Aazad, who in turn through his eyes gestured to not utter a word. But Rudra went on and said, "He had feelings for you. He loved you. But did not have the courage to express the same. I thought it was one-sided until that day, when we three met for the first time same place. That day I realized even you had feelings for him and like dumb even you didn't express or even worse, had no idea about it."

After all the drama that unfolded in the last 15-20 minutes, came an absolute silence all of a sudden. Nobody uttered anything. Rudra sat on his chair and continued to feel sad about the incomplete love story. While Aazad and Krisha exchanged dialogues through eyes.

Aazad where on one hand felt ashamed and guilty of Rudra's behavior and apologized through his eyes; Krisha on the other hand could not digest of the fact that Aazad let her go this easily. She also blamed herself of not realizing what she felt and was shocked to see- Rudra coming to know of her feelings at the debut meet.

The unsaid and the unspoken pinched harder than Rudra's expressions. Breaking the ice, Krisha said with agony, "We are here to discuss your love interest and not anybody else's. Got that Mr. Rudra!" She threw her words at Rudra but it was directed to hit Aazad. And Aazad very well understood the same by her deeds.

In a dejected tone she continued, "So can we discuss for which we have assembled here or are we going to talk rubbish for the remaining time? Aazad shall we discuss or you want to speak something?"

Aazad just gestured moving his head sideways and signaled of not having anything to speak. Krisha on seeing the denial gesture from Aazad was in disbelief. She stayed shocked and could not believe of Aazad still not speaking his heart out.

Keeping aside the personal story, Krisha started, "So getting back to business let me tell you, Adrija had a very troubled past. Firstly, she witnessed her father's death, followed by rejection from Anand, then there was a break up due to long distance relationship and death of a best friend due to covid-19. These are few major instances that has impacted her mental well-being extremely."

"And what about her dad thing? She has been hallucinating him since I have known her and possibly even before that," said Rudra.

"Well as I already told, Adrija has seen a lot of lows too early in her life. She appears to make her deceased father as a source to share every little thing happening in her life, who sadly don't exist. And which is why I am insisting on her treatment," replied Krisha.

"Can this be a potential danger? I mean, can it cause harm to her or to the society in long term, if left untreated or we delay the treatment? Especially, as and when she ages, meet new people and weave relationships?" asked Rudra in a little nervy tone.

"I cannot assure but it needs to be treated for sure. But yes there has been one thing that has been bothering the most," replied Krisha.

"And that is?" finally Aazad got himself involved yet again after all the melodrama.

Krisha gave a venomous look and sent a message of dare not speak through her eyes. And she answered in alarmed tone, "Her nature seems to have turned violent which is clearly reflected through her handwriting and especially those THE END's. All the more, this has been progressive as she grew older."

"Violent nature indicates what? I mean anything to worry?" asked Rudra now seeming to get uncomfortable and his expressions turning unpleasant.

"Well in a way yes. I will be frank and open, will not hide anything. In such cases the person either harms himself/herself or the ones who have caused trouble in their lives. Also, the extent to which they can be harmful, can only be decided by knowing the background in depth and having that person for one to one session," replied Krisha with utmost transparency.

This created a stir in the atmosphere and the environment did not appear calm, ever again. After hearing this, both boys felt as if their ears had begun to bled, the ground trembled beneath the feet and inner peace went for a toss.

A mere diary had turned their lives upside down and were clueless of how to go about this further. Aazad was merely a part of this but Rudra; he was horrified and seemed to have reached the dead end, unfortunately having no U-Turn. They were in an absolute state of shock. None had the braveries to take this conversation further and perspired heavily.

Seeing the two in trauma, Krisha said, "Well I would recommend to get Adrija here for a session and then decide the further course of action."

The two remained unspoken. There was not a single word uttered. It felt as if both had seen a ghost or were possessed by a spirit that held them from talking. Krisha stood behind in a gap between both the chairs and kept a hand each on both the boys shoulder. To which they reacted frightfully and terrorized they said in sync, "We wish to leave. Please let us go," they pleaded with folded hands.

"Running away is not a solution. You Rudra? You wanted to share rest of your life with her, right? What happened all of a sudden? Just because she is not well mentally, you wish to leave her? I told you, Adrija began to feel better after meeting you. Also, I am sure you must have not experienced any such episode, which is why you are with her till date and want to commit yourself for rest of your life," said Krisha infusing hope, positivity and cheering him up.

"I so love her and there are no doubts about it. But this violence and rebellious nature kind of a person is not my type. I so wished for her to get fine from the very first day and you very well know about it. But, what I just heard has shattered me from inside and left me in splits," replied Rudra as he continued to shiver.

"So you want her to get back to her ancient days and face another heartbreak. Let me tell you, it is because of people like you in her past that has led to these kind of atrocities and shambled her inner soul away from her," told Krisha as she felt for poor Adrija.

"I am clueless. Fine tell me what do you want me to do. In no ways I want her to go back from where she has rose and that too with such difficulty," replied Rudra in an under-confident dejected tenor.

"There are two possibilities-

1.   Get her here and treat her for her current situation. But would be very difficult as you have not told her of secretly getting her diary.

2.   Get in to her past and explore all that has occurred in her childhood. And take my opinion, her mother will be the most correct person to help you on this. You just somehow need to get to her and rest of the story will go forward in the smoothest possible way," said Krisha.

"We should now turn spies to investigate her past? We are no cops nor any detectives to get into all this. What rubbish? Just treat her for the present illness and rest should be okay," intervened Aazad feeling stupid of the second suggestion and denying it upfront.

"How much do you know about what love is? I can get it why you did not approach me. You are scared of putting efforts in a relationship. So keep your mouth shut and stop influencing a friend who is willing to take a right call," replied Krisha with utmost fire and rage.

"I feel second option is good. I know her Bihar address. Once we reach there, it will be easier for us to find her mother and then work on other stories," mediated Rudra.

Aazad nodded out of dismay and felt Rudra making a big mistake by going Krisha's way (as suggested). However, Krisha was happy with Rudra's decision and getting the smile back on her face positively said, "I feel you personally going and investigating would not be that great of an idea."

"Then?" asked Rudra.

"I can help you with a private detective's address. You can meet him and take this forward. And to your knowledge he has a 100 percent success ratio," replied Krisha confidently.

"Please do the needful," replied Rudra seeking for help and himself realizing the suggestion being a better option.

Krisha wrote the address on a piece of paper and gave it to Rudra. Rudra thanked her for the same and the two boys decided to leave. As they reached exit, they heard Krisha saying loud and clear, "If there is anything, just call me directly, no need to involve third person in middle of all this."

Aazad heard and left with a heavy heart. Rudra tried to console but Aazad was broken from inside.

CHAPTER 6

DETECTIVE CHANDU RAY

Aazad and Rudra stood outside an old building, in the busy streets of Byculla, Mumbai. They gazed at the structure for about a minute and common thought ran across the minds- the construction being so ancient, gave a feeling that it could fall at any given point of time. The surroundings so filthy that they could not stand the bad odour coming from the chawl. The very presence of the two at the given address, gave them the feeling of being ridiculed. Both appeared frustrated with this kind of recommendation by Dr. Krisha.

"First your friend Krisha, and now this. What are we up to Aazad? Do you think we can get some help from this stinking low class site?" asked Rudra.

"I am nowhere to be blamed. It is you, who agreed on having all this investigated. Now what? Well, keeping everything aside you need to be patient and not appear impulsive on everything. Patience is the key to success," replied Aazad keeping it short and sweet. Also showing some faith in Krisha's reference, though the last meet had bitterness exchanged between the two.

"Oh yes. I saw the result of you being patient. Krisha got along with someone else, and that too for a lifetime. I request, you at least don't talk about patience," taunted Rudra.

"You are being personal. Mind it," replied Aazad out of anger.

"I am sorry for that, but what kind of friends she has? What is this place? I am surprised. Krisha being a doctor and keeping such contacts puts me in a fix. Moreover, she recommending such place gives me a feeling of some kind of syndicate leading to mishap rather than being helpful" said Rudra out of bewilderment.

"Oh is it? When I suggested to not get down into this muddle, both of you turned deaf ears and enjoyed ignoring me. Now, when you sense you are stuck, you feel silly of her advice and suddenly she is all my friend. Wow! You hypocrite!" replied Aazad with a sarcasm.

On hearing Aazad's reply, Rudra kept his head down and did not react.

"Now that we are here, we should at least explore what's stored for us in the box? You never know, it might surprise us by having the good waiting for us! Let us experience the man behind the doors of room number 7 and then draw a conclusion. Shall we?" asked Aazad gathering all the possible good vibes that he could, despite the not so good-looking scenario.

Rudra in return just nodded and showed some faith in Aazad's positive marketing. The two started approaching the antique structure. The closer they got to the destination, the more it made Rudra feel disgusted about their presence. Surprisingly, even Aazad had begun to lose his faith and the ever boasting confidence began to enter into the dull conclave.

As it is rightly said, love is blind and Aazad being no different, was the real reason that had his hopes afloat. This being Krisha's personal recommendation, pushed him to move forward, albeit against his own will.

After completing a distance of more than 500 meters and climbing three floors; finally, the two reached the desired room. Breathless and putting efforts to get some oxygen, Rudra read the room number and disappointed he said, "What the hell is this 007?

The person thinks himself of being some James Bond? Aazad I cannot believe that you still wanna be part of this mockery!"

"Can you for once, keep your mouth shut and trust. I felt gimmicky even when you agreed to Krisha's suggestion of discovering the truth about Adrija. And going all the way to Bihar for the same, appeared even more foolish to me. I mean who does that? Who the hell has so much time? Still, I agreed to come with you today and now you want to get back without meeting? Just stay quiet and let us meet this person. One more senseless reaction from you and I shall leave," replied Aazad losing his temper.

"Ok. Cool down and relax. I totally get that. Chill. Can we now knock at the James Bond's gate and see the man behind this access?" said Rudra not irritating Aazad any further.

Aazad nodded. Just when Aazad raised his hand, the door opened before his fingers made any contact with the wooden gate. And the man inside greeted the two, "Welcome to Chandu Ray's paradise please come in."

Chandu- The name perfectly synchronized with the kind of personality he had. The man in his late thirties had a very ordinary appearance. Around 163cms of height, dark complexion, bald head, French beard and a thick round shaped soda glasses as eyewear. Talking of his attire- he wore a long loose white shirt reaching the knees (kurta), a black pajama and a black modi jacket with the buttons left open.

Rudra and Aazad glared at the character. Almost after a gaze of 30 seconds, Aazad whispered, "He appears more of a poet to me than a detective."

"Oh no you can't say this. Your miss Krisha has referred the person, so let's get in and have some fun," murmured Rudra in his satirical best.

"Are you guys talking something? I guess, you must be talking of how I got to know about your existence at the door. Well this is what I am known for- my sixth sense. I come to know about things before they occur. One of my qualities, obviously out of a list of many. Please come in," said Chandu and smiled. Out of all the ordinaries, his smile was most extra-ordinary. He had protruding front teeth (bunny tooth structure) that were highlighted immediately and it could no way be missed.

Looking at the smile the two laughed, "Surely you do Chandu ji. You are absolutely great and miraculous," said Rudra pulling Chandu's leg without him knowing about the same. And the two entered the house.

Being called as the paradise at the welcome, appeared as a shocker to both upon entering. The room almost ended as soon as they entered, as in- it was no bigger than 150 square feet. It just had a charpoy, a chair, a center table, a water filter with some glasses and two 6 feet tall double door cupboards. The entire setting appeared very congested and gave a feeling of claustrophobic.

"You don't eat and excrete? I mean I see no kitchen, no washroom and also you don't bathe?" asked Aazad out of disappointment. Rudra was shocked to see him this blunt and straight-forward. This hinted at Aazad being really pissed of what was presented in front of him in the name of 'so-called detective.'

"I do eat but outside, as I am mostly on-field for investigation purpose. Coming to your doubt of bathing and expelling, then we have a common toilet at the entrance of the society to the left," replied Chandu and he smiled again.

Looking at the smile Rudra and Aazad giggled yet again and found it really funny of him doing the same. They were enjoying the man's antics and the way he displayed his over the top character.

"Well, let's talk about the case now? What do you want out of me? I mean how can I help you in solving the unsolvable?" asked Chandu.

"Well there is this girl called Adrija, and I want you to carry out her background check. Find everything about her past, search about the present and look for her family members," replied Rudra.

"C'mon friend don't be shy. She's not just any friend but your girlfriend. Nobody does this background check for any girl. This only happens if you are interested and want to be sure if everything has been alright in the past. Am I sounding right or absolutely right?" asked Chandu.

"Woahhh. Right or absolutely right- this is some kind of new to me. I have heard about the opposite with the right, but this is different," intervened Aazad.

"This is Chandu's charm. You will fail to find elsewhere and for the same reason you are here. The reason that I am distinctive and unique," replied Chandu with all sense of pride in his tenor.

"Gosh! This man is a package of over-confidence and stupid antics," whispered Rudra getting closer to Aazad.

"You want to ask something? Ask me direct and let me show you my intellect," interjected Chandu.

"Easy man. Apply brakes to your claims. I just want an answer to a simple question- Can you help?" asked Rudra.

"For sure. You know," as Chandu continued to speak.

And Rudra interrupted and stopped Chandu "Enough I got my answer, now can we talk business."

"Yes please. First provide me some basic details about the girl. Like, where to begin and how to go about the same," asked Chandu in a grumbled tone.

"To begin with your investigation you will have to go to Bihar. Her roots are in Patna. She was born and brought up there, did her schooling and stayed until 2018. Since then she has been staying here in Mumbai and studying in Girls College. So once you close the Bihar investigation, you come back to Mumbai and collect the left over pieces of the puzzle. And finally report us," explained Rudra.

"Bihaaaaaarrrrr… It is too far and I can't even take my car," dramatic Chandu replied.

"Don't be poetic and dramatic. Will you do it or not?" asked Aazad.

"Of course! There is nothing that Chandu can't do. My name is Chandu Ray and to find truth is my work, all night and day," replied Chandu in a firm voice.

"Were you a poet or are you still the one?" asked Aazad.

"I am still the one, but only in my leisure time. And sadly I don't have any free time so I keep using these one-liners. My very own creatives," said Chandu.

"I told you this man looks more of a poet than a detective. Let's leave, it's not his cup of tea. He is impossible and can't be the right person for the task," a disgusted Aazad told Rudra.

"Excuse me I bet on it, you will not find a better poet than me," said Chandu. On hearing the confession, the two men were taken aback and this validated their feeling of being at the wrong place.

Seeing the expressions of the two deteriorate further, Chandu realized his subconscious mistake and took a pause before speaking anything further. Soon he said, "Sorry that was a slip of tongue. I meant you will not find a better private detective than me, in the entire country."

The two boys still differed. They believed all he said was no more than a jargon and hardly showed any improvement on their facial lexes. Chandu continued his own furor, "Okay let us have it this way. You just pay for my travel tickets and that too one sided, rest all will be taken care by me. I will carry out the investigation, do my job and get back with the desired info. Upon completion, you guys decide whether I was good at it or not, and pay. If I fail to reach the expected level, then do not pay me. Also, I shall return that one sided fare. Sounds good?"

The claim was huge and the risk that Chandu was ready to take, was even bigger. This somewhat brew confidence in the two men sitting out there and they seemed to get convinced a bit. From all the conversations that occurred till now, it all appeared casual and some kind of a gimmick, but this time Rudra and Aazad saw the stimulus in Chandu's eyes.

"Trust me. There is nothing for you two to lose. If you want I can sign and give you in writing on a piece of paper," said Chandu with weightage.

This was like a last nail in the coffin and Chandu at last emerged successful in convincing the two. "No need to give anything in written. We somewhat trust you and are shocked by ourselves as we say this. But yes it's a deal," said Rudra.

"In case you are good at it and give us the desired data, then what will be the fee? I mean how much do you charge per case?" asked Aazad.

"I charge fifty thousand per case that too locally. But this being an intercity case, you will have to pay me a fee of 1 lac plus the traveling, food and my accommodation expense," replied a poised Chandu.

The eye-balls popped out on hearing the charges. The fact that he charged this heavily per case and stayed in an unacceptable condition got them to disbelief. On hearing the fees, Aazad said, "You charge handsomely and stay miserably. I must say either you don't get cases or you think we are some fools to believe in you."

"This is what I charge. If it's fine with you, then we may proceed; or else that's the door for the exit, you two may leave," replied Chandu in a way things making only sense for the very first time.

"Ouch! That hurt. You were pretty rude," said Aazad looking at the all new avatar of Chandu.

"Well I tried to be courteous but you found it foolish. So I showed you my true colors. You like or dislike, my fee remains non-negotiable. But my deal very much stays valid," replied Chandu with all intensity.

Aazad and Rudra were amazed by Chandu's outburst. The

serious side of him sounded rather lethal and the two were totally blown away.

"Ok. Chandu it's a deal. When do we begin?" asked Rudra offering a handshake with an intent of seal the deal.

"At the earliest," replied Chandu accepting the handshake.

The two got out of the chawl and their acuity changed after the last 10 minutes spent with Chandu. Surprised Rudra said, "I was shocked to see him in that fervor. I am rarely wrong in identifying people, but I must accept- I made a mistake in recognizing two talented individuals on both occasions. This is a rarity and I hardly fail, but yes I was unsuccessful in both Krisha and Chandu's case. My perception has significantly changed and I can rightly call them both as- Geniuses."

Hearing this Aazad had a huge laugh and said, "Are you kidding me? You are good at recognizing people? Seriously? And let me tell you, you did not miss on two, rather you completed the hat-trick of misconceptions with Chandu."

Confused about what Aazad really intended, Rudra asked, "What do you mean?"

Aazad continued to giggle and said, "What I mean is ADRIJA! She is your biggest mistake (out of the three) and you have failed miserably in knowing her. You were and never are good at understanding people and which is why we are in a mess. I did not share my feelings with Krisha is a mistake, I get it. But you expressing yours to Adrija is a bigger mistake. And still wandering in hope of things to get normal is even more wrong."

Rudra failed to reply. He already appeared confused and failed to identify the correct way out in dealing the situation; and Aazad all the more sounded demoralizing. But he knew one thing with absolute determination, that his love for Adrija was unconditional. Thus he remained mum with heads down and continued to go ahead with Chandu-plan.

CHAPTER 7

THE BIHAR INVESTIGATION

Detective Chandu left for Bihar 3 days after the meet with the boys. He was on a roll and appeared animated to find the truth; more so as the boys found him incapable and gimmicky. It was a tough challenge, but Chandu being himself- nothing short of confidence and fortitude. By the way, it was also his first case towards north-eastern side of India, which added to his exhilaration.

After a tiring journey of 34 hours, Chandu finally stepped on the soil of Patna. As he breathed in the fresh atmosphere of Patna, came a smell of typical Patna and things what it is known for.

Patna- a sacred terrestrial land that stretches along the south bank of Ganges River and is a capital to Bihar. Known for its holiness, it is famous as the land of Gods, having ancient Buddhist, Hindu and Jain pilgrimage centres of Vaishali, Rajgir, Nalanda, Bodh Gaya and Pawapuri. Also it is a sanctified city for Sikhs as the tenth Sikh *Guru- Guru Shri Gobind Singh ji* was born here.

There was so much to explore on visiting Patna and Chandu had no different plans. He was happy to be here and had all plans of wandering around, but case was primary and exploration being secondary. On getting out of the railway station, Chandu first found himself an accommodation and was on a roll, subsequently.

To begin with, he had this Patna address of Adrija where the family resided. After getting friendly with the Patna climate and its beautiful environment, he straightaway headed to the given address and kick-started the investigation.

JHA'S, HOUSE NO. 11, Jagdeo Path, Ashokpuri, Patna, Bihar 800014. On reaching the given address, Chandu stood confused as rest of the things matched except 'THE NAME' on the name plate, which displayed 'YADAV'S'. He continued to stay still and scratched his head for the next five minutes, until he approached a passing pedestrian, "Excuse me madam."

The lady stopped on the approach and replied, "Yes bhaiya. How can I help? I saw you from far (as I bought vegetables), waiting at the gate and looking for something. Also, you don't seem like a local. Tell me how can I help?"

"Ji didi (sister), you are right. I have come from Mumbai to meet a friend of mine and invite her for a wedding," replied Chandu.

"Oh nice! Who is it? Your son or daughter? Who is getting married?" asked the lady out of excitement.

Annoyed he instantly replied, "I am getting married."

The lady was shocked on hearing the reply. She gave a top to bottom stare to the man and stood in disbelief. The appearance that Chandu had of his typical long shirt, pyjama and modi jacket with soda glasses on, gave a jolt to the lady of him getting married. Ignoring the reply, she joked, "Poor girl" and laughed out loud.

This filled Chandu with anger and he so wanted to burst out at the lady, but keeping the need of the moment in mind, he faked calmness and said, "Madam can you please help. I have the same address and to my knowledge JHA's resided here. But now as I see it is YADAV's name etched on the nameplate. Please help. Rest of the details like venue and all I will share later. Also, I would invite you to the wedding along with the travel tickets fully sponsored by me."

The invitation thing brought a huge smile on the lady's face and happily she responded, "I reside in this locality since 2001 and as far as I remember, Jha ji's daughter sold the property five years back and left the city. Since then, the Yadav's have been the owners of the property."

"What about Mrs. Jha? I know Jha ji died in an accident, but what about Adrija's mother?" asked Chandu as he stayed staggered.

"Oh Kaavya! She lost her life in another accident just a year after Piyush Ji died. Poor girl (Adrija) stayed all alone, managed studies and all other stuff by herself. Finally, frustrated of the loneliness, Adrija sold everything she had here and left for another city. This is what I feel. I pity that little girl, how unfortunate can life be and Adrija being the perfect example," replied the lady in a saddened tone, continuing to feel for Adrija.

Chandu's ears stood up alarmed on hearing the reply and he felt devastated. The hope of getting something on the visit to Bihar now appeared indistinct. This feeling for Chandu, was similar to the batsman returning to the pavilion on a golden duck (like in the game of cricket). All his energies suddenly fell flat and he turned absolute blank. His first step forward had backlashed and sadly there was no any plan B or an alternate start point.

"Oh hello bhaiya. What happened you alright? You said your friend stayed here, I thought they were from Yadav family. But now I feel you came here for the Jha's. Hello, bhaiya I am talking to you, are you listening?" and the lady continued to poke Chandu repeatedly.

"How much can you rattle on aunty? Can you keep your blabbering mouth shut for some time and let the other person think? Since the time I have stopped you, you have been emitting shit out of your oral aperture. Give me a break," replied Chandu out of infuriation and irritation.

Hearing the same the lady felt deeply hurt and was in tears instantaneously. Seeing the lady cry, Chandu panicked and out of uneasiness said, "Sorry. Sorry. Didi please don't cry. I am just tensed as I came here for something and discovered a different story, altogether. Please didi understand I just vented out of anger and did not mean on hurting you. Please didi, please I am new to this place. Stop crying, onlookers will take it otherwise and it will spoil my visit to this place," begged Chandu, as he saw people around gawking the two and especially Chandu.

Chandu shivered as long as the lady cried. After consoling and buttering the lady for few minutes, she stopped crying and said, "First assure, you will call me to your wedding. As it is this invitation is getting wasted because you could not meet the Jha's, so why not invite me and my husband instead? This will free you from the guilt and make me also happy."

Chandu could not believe to what the lady said and faking he also agreed. "Sure. But you will have to help me with one thing," said Chandu.

Smilingly the lady said, "Yes ask."

"Can you tell me anything about the Jha's that would help me to find or discover something solid about the family? I mean Adrija's schooling, college, whatever you know!" said Chandu trying his luck in this hopeless condition.

To this the lady instantly replied, "Adrija went to Patna Public School along with my daughter. Also, she was great at academics so she went to Prof. Anand Kumar's Scholars Academy for private coaching. This is all I know and there is nothing to help beyond this."

Finally, this came as a silver lining and Chandu with some smile on his face replied, "Thank you didi. I have not printed my wedding card yet, also the bride is yet to be found. The groom is ready and raring to go, but rest of the things are yet to be arranged. As soon as, rest of the things get decided, I will send you the invitation. I am in search of something. Keep this card and let me know, if anything important pops up or you remember something. But promise, I will call you to my wedding," with this Chandu began to walk ahead without waiting for the lady to react.

The lady found the man weird and upon seeing the card she realized of him being a private detective and not any relative of the Jha's. She stood for a minute in suspicion, wondering the reason behind the man's investigation. However, least bothered about the search but heart-broken, she soon left with a gloomy face (on being fooled about the wedding).

Chandu quickly rushed to the Scholar's Academy. On reaching the academy, "Excuse me, where is the office?" asked Chandu to the security guard at the building entrance.

"Second floor to the right of the staircase, room no. 29" replied the guard.

Thanking the man, Chandu climbed the staircase in haste. He hurriedly found room no. 29. Chandu looked at the top which had a name board hanging, that read Mr. Kumar. The door of the cabin remained open and waiting at the entrance, he saw a man (roughly) in early-forties seated on the chair. Knocking at the door of the room he asked, "May I come in?"

The man positioned on the chair saw through the spectacles, stressing his eyes and getting the eyebrows closer. Unable to recognize, Kumar asked in a heavy tenor, "What do you want? Who are you?"

Without being permitted to enter, Chandu started approaching the man's table. Seeing this, Mr. Kumar felt uneasy and said, "Hello why the hell are you coming inside? I asked- what do you want and did not allow you in."

Chandu however did not stop and continued to the table. On reaching the same, he pulled the chair out and sat. This made Mr. Kumar uncomfortable and he continued to find the man strange.

Chandu soon got up (even before he could make himself comfortable), forcefully held Mr. Kumar's hand and said, "I am so thankful that you are here, Anand Kumar ji. You don't know how terrible I felt before coming here. Absolutely grateful."

Mr. Kumar pulled back his hand and said, "Have you lost it, completely? I am not Anand. And who the hell let you in? And why you wish to meet Anand? I have never seen you before, who are you?"

"The plate outside mentioned Mr. Kumar. If you are not Anand then why the hell have you occupied his seat. Where is Anand Kumar? Call him. I have come all the way from Mumbai to meet. And for God's sake, stop wasting my time. You have no idea how much have I suffered before reaching here," replied Chandu in-turn reprimanding the other Kumar.

This kind of misbehavior irked Mr. Kumar and out of anguish he gave back, "Mumbai? We have never been to that place, FYI. And you being his friend, you don't know that Anand is no more. What rubbish claims, just get up and get out. You appear a threat to this premises, walk out willingly or I shall call the security."

And another shocker gripped Chandu. His ears heard the most miserable thing, which surely they would have never wished. This appeared like a live nightmare for Chandu and splintered he sat numb. He wished to re-confirm on what he just heard and asked, "No more meaning?"

"Get your ass out of the cabin. You don't know what does that mean? He is not alive anymore. Now you get it? Now get out and stop creating a fuss," said Kumar fumingly and unable to control his temper.

Seeing Kumar losing his calm, Chandu quickly took out his visiting card and placed it on the table in front of Kumar. Kumar picked up the same and read it loud, "Detective Chandu Ray. Private investigator and spy. What nonsense is this?"

Chandu still trying to recuperate (although unable to, even after trying hard) said in desolation, "Look Kumar, I will come straight to the point. I am here to find out the truth behind Piyush Jha's death. There has been something unusual about the incident that night and I have been appointed by Mumbai Police (of course off the record) to collect information. So I have been trying to reach as many individuals as possible that can help in solving the mystery."

Kumar found the reason bizarre, but still tried to help and replied, "I don't know how can I help in this scenario. Neither do I know any Piyush, nor am I able to connect with what you say. Tell me straight and bold, what do you want from here?"

Chandu counted something on his fingers. He calculated something which was evident from his face. He nodded in one moment and then disagreed with himself in the other. He continued to do so and after a few seconds of thinking, he said, "Adrija is now what 23-24. This being an academy for 10th grade students, she might have studied here somewhere between 2013-2015. Please check for this student Adrija Jha and then only you can offer some help."

Tired of this detective's antics, frustrated Kumar said, "I am not any directory service provider to help you on this. Just get lost."

"Just 15 minutes. Just give me 15 minutes, please understand and treat this as important as somebody's life. Please co-operate sir and I would be gone the sixteenth minute," assured Chandu, trying to convince Kumar.

Kumar somehow appeared to melt and hearing the man's ply, he turned to the desktop. He typed something and after couple of minutes, "Here you go. Oh yes I remember this girl, she was brilliant and record-breaker for our institute. Nobody has been able to surpass her grades till date. Adrija was a darling to all of us and especially to Anand," said Kumar, thus providing some relief to Chandu.

Chandu on getting the information, immediately got up and went to the other side of the table and peeped into the desktop. On matching all things correctly, he asked, "When did Anand Kumar die?"

"It has been over 5 years and we continue to grieve the loss of this great man. Every brick of this institute has his name etched all over. It was only Anand's vision that has got this academy to a position where it is today. We are not in the league with any other coaching centers, rather we have created a legacy of our own, all thanks to the Legendary Anand Kumar," replied Kumar with a heavy heart.

This description somehow appeared fake to Chandu. He felt this explanation been thrown at him, just because Chandu introduced himself being appointed by the police. Chandu was no less in over-acting, hence replicating Kumar's expressions he said, "There is nothing that can be done against the natural force. It is HE (referring to GOD) who decides the birth and death of an individual. It is inevitable."

Kumar ignored the falsified condolences given to him and kept quiet.

Coming out of the zone, Chandu asked, "How did Anand Kumar die?"

"That is none of your business and how is that even related to this?" replied Kumar.

"Answer me or I shall report to the police that you were non-cooperative," said Chandu in a threatening tone.

Looking at the fierce side of Chandu, Kumar felt threatened and spoke, "Anand Kumar died due to heart attack in the year 2017. Anand being a fitness freak, this kind of death came as a shocker to all of us. But as you said, we are helpless in front of Almighty, we felt the same on his departure."

Chandu felt this story unconvincing and not without hiccups. There was something between the lines that was not seen, but existed. Amazed he asked, "What did the doctors say? Like did you guys go for an autopsy or something or just performed the last rites?"

"What autopsy? He died a natural death at the center. He was rushed to the hospital as he fell on the floor while teaching, but immediately declared dead upon arrival. He was waved off like others are cremated. The only good thing was- he took his last breath here at the center- the place where it all started and at his foundation. He must have rested in peace by breathing the last breath at the institute," replied Kumar.

Chandu understood of things turning futile for him and that Kumar was done with his side of story. Thus, without wasting any further time Chandu abruptly got up and said, "Thank you Mr. Kumar for giving your time. It was not such a pleasure meeting you. I must say, the information shared has not been of any help and you have come across as a big disappointment to me. Good bye!" With this Chandu left the cabin,without hearing Kumar's reply.

Kumar found this weird and felt disgusted. However, he did not pay heed to the conversation and continued with his work. Chandu on the other hand roamed the entire campus and tried if he could collect something, but in vain.

Leaving the academy, he took his investigation forward by visiting Patna Public School. He tried hard on getting his hands on something solid but returned with the persistent void. He had tit-bit of data but nothing substantial.

After 3 days of rigorous analysis and research, Chandu stood dissatisfied on the 4th day morning in his hotel room. Standing in front of a 3x2 feet wooden structure, where he stuck notes (in which he had jotted all the data that he had collected about Adrija), Chandu was unable to connect the dots. "How can there not be anything about Adrija? There is something I am failing at and unable to get, which is why these dots appear disconnected. I need to find the missing link," murmured Chandu to himself, as he remained dazed.

After grinding the grey matter for over 15 minutes, churning the thoughts that bumped randomly in his cerebrum and combating a battle between heart and his mind, he popped up, "Let's go back to where it all began. I am sure Yadav's might be aware of something. Nobody, would buy such a huge property from a stranger and that too from a little girl. Yes, let me investigate the Yadav's."

Hurryingly, Chandu got out of his nightwear and slipped into his usual kurta-pyjama attire. He headed straight to the Yadva's residence and in no time he was seen standing at the entrance gate. Chandu took a deep breath and waited (for about 5 minutes, thinking) at the gate before doing anything further.

"Excuse me. Hello security, excuse. I need to meet Yadav Ji," called Chandu through the gaps in the wooden gate, trying to interact with the security guard.

"Who are you? Saahab doesn't meet anybody without appointment. Get back and leave," the security guard replied from the cabin.

"I am Chandu, I have his appointment. Just tell him Chandu has come down all the way from Mumbai to invite him for the wedding," replied a fidgety Chandu through the gaps, as doors were yet to open for him.

Security guard gave a suspicious stare to the guy but still on not knowing the man, he thought of taking a chance by calling Mr. Yadav. The guard called from his cabin, "Sir, some Chandu has come from Mumbai to meet you."

"Who the hell is Chandu? I don't know any such person. Don't call me for stupid strangers taking my name, Narayan. Or I shall screw you. Keep the phone down. I am already frenzied by Mrs. Yadav and her demands, just don't call me for anybody whom you don't know," and Mr. Yadav kept the telephone receiver in anguish.

On keeping the call, Narayan came with red eyes towards the gate and in all agony said, "Just get lost or I shall hit you with this rod (pointing at the wooden stick he had in his cabin). Mumbai huh? Because of you I heard from sir. Buzz off before I get pissed and break your bones. I should have had understood from your dressing sense itself. My bad, bloody beggar."

Chandu realized his wedding trick falling flat this time and could sense the endangering vibes. Without any further conversation, he decided to wait on the opposite side of the road.

On seeing him wait, the guard screamed on top of his voice, "Just get out of my sight. I should not see you anywhere near this premises."

Chandu in turn replied with fury, "This street is not Yadav's personal property, the bungalow is. And you are no guard to this public road, so mind your fucking business or I shall call the cops."

Narayan stepped behind without uttering and got back to the cabin. Chandu on the other hand kept murmuring, "Bloody idiots. They think, they own the entire country. They don't even let individuals breathe easy at public places. Morons."

After the scuffle, Chandu continued to wait on the road, sitting under a tree to avoid the heat. After an hour (almost) he saw a car coming out of the gate. Chandu ran behind the car for few meters but then it accelerated beyond his reach. Narayan saw and commented with a wicked grin, "Good chase, but you need to be as fast as a beast to reach. Bloody stray animal."

Chandu heard it all but ignored and positioned himself back, under the tree. After, a while he saw a lady walking out of the gate, he stood up excitedly. Chandu followed the lady but maintaining a good distance yelled, "Hello, madam. Hello, Mrs. Yadav, hello."

The lady turned for once but ignored and kept walking. Chandu did not follow for long (out of ethics) and disappointed, came back to his original waiting zone.

Right after ten minutes he saw a girl faraway approaching the gate. This time he decided to go a little ahead, down the road and wait behind a barricade (positioned about 400-500 meters away from the bungalow).

As Chandu reached the barricade, a bike came and stopped near the barrier. The man (rider) on the bike, waited with his helmet on. The girl brisk walked towards the bike. As she neared the vehicle, she kept turning back; probably to make sure nobody followed her. On reaching to a distance of less than a meter, she ran towards the bike and sat, gesturing the guy to leave asap.

The girl's facial expressions exhibited fear and it was clearly evident. Taking this as an opportunity and banking on the same, Chandu like a phantom suddenly appeared right in front of the two-wheeler and said, "Hmmmm… Boyfriend! Your dad knows about this?"

"Oh no please, don't tell him, he will lock me in a room and I cannot live without this guy," the little girl panicked and begged for nondisclosure.

"Don't worry I won't, but only if you help me," replied Chandu.

"Help you with what? Are you trying to blackmail?" the guy interrupted.

"No. I want to know little bit about Adrija. This is serious and a must. Please help. I don't want to interfere in your personal matter nor am I interested, but need help. Please help I beg," said Chandu with folded hands asking for assistance.

The girl appeared stunned and nervy on hearing Adrija's name. She came close to Chandu and said, "How do you know her? And why are you asking about her after such a long gap? Is she alright? This doesn't give me any good vibes."

"She is fine but I need to know about her past. It is not her but someone else's life in danger. So please share whatever you know about her; if possible please highlight the minutest details," replied Chandu trying to calm the girl down.

"Are you mad? Talking such sensitive things in front of him," whispered the girl pointing towards his guy. "Dheeraj you continue to college. I will see you there in a while. Also, please keep this as a secret," continued the girl and asked Dheeraj to leave.

The guy left and Chandu along with the girl went to a coffee shop nearby. As they sat, Chandu asked, "What is your name and how do you know Adrija?"

"I am Naina and we studied together in Junior college (in class 11th & 12th). We were best of the friends during those two years," replied the girl.

"Continue I am listening please don't stop. I don't have much of a time. Please I beg," pleaded Chandu.

"Okay. We became friends through a weird connection. She had this friend of hers named Naina. But somehow they broke connection as Naina moved to another city. Her father was in some corporate company and took transfer to another city, hence the entire family shifted to Pune. This might be when she was appearing in 10th."

"Excuse me sir, mam, your order please," interrupted the coffee shop's waiter.

Chandu in a disgusted tone, "Ummmm, Mr.... what's your name? Yes, Mr. Adil (reading the nametag on the chest), don't you see we are in a middle of an important conversation."

"I am so sorry to bother you both sir, but you need to place an order," replied Adil.

"It's ok, One cappuccino for me, sugar separate. And you Naina?"

"One macchiato for me. The regular one with sugar in it," ordered Naina.

"Thank you sir, madam, have a beautiful time," said the waiter and left.

"What did he mean by beautiful time? Do we look like a couple to him?" asked Naina in a petrified manner.

"Why should we think what Adil thinks? You continue on the story. What after the Pune shifting?" questioned Chandu.

Naina regained her composure and said, "It was the first day of our college. Everyone was introducing self, when called for attendance. My turn came and as soon as I introduced myself as Naina, Adrija turned at me with widened eyeballs. She continued to stare as I spoke and till the time I spoke; making me feel really uneasy. Once I finished with my introduction and was about to seat, she gave me a smile. I felt of this action being vague and absolutely avoided her for the next few days," replied Naina.

"Cappuccino for you sir, minus the sugar. These are your sugar sachets, one each of white and brown. Hope you enjoy the coffee," Adil interjected.

Chandu maintained silence but spoke through his eyes and warned Adil. Sadly, Adil left without noticing the gesture.

Naina continued, "One day during the lunch break, she came to my table and said-

"Look I know you must be feeling awkward of me giving you those stares, but trust me your name reminds me of my friend whose name also happens to be Naina. And before you feel of me faking the same, look at this," and she showed me Naina's display picture (DP) on YourBuddy (an application). And three-four photos of their meet."

I saw the same and was amused to find that she (Naina) actually resembled me. And it was not a mere one, the match was more than fifty percent. It left me in splits and with no other option but to believe that Adrija had no reason to fake. She further told me the stories of their friendship and how cordial their camaraderie was. I melted. From that very day we gelled really well and I sort of replaced the gone Naina in Adrija's life. We became best of friends and began to share every bit of our lives like our past, present, who all existed in our lives and imparted every little info," said Naina.

"Your macchiato madam with sugar. I am keeping extra sachets along, just in case you want to sweeten the bitter brew. Enjoy madam," Adil interrupted yet again.

This time Chandu lost his cool and said, "How do you get to know that we have reached an important juncture in the story.

And at an absolute turning point, you arise out of nowhere like a batman. How man? How do you not fail to interrupt us at the wrong time?"

"Excuse me Sir, that's my job," replied Adil.

"To interfere is your job? Seriously? Then take my advice you should change your job?" replied Chandu getting red in the face.

"Excuse me. To serve the hot-coffee hot is my job, I got nothing to do with your story uncle," returned Adil in turn beginning to lose his temper.

The uncle sentence made Naina giggle and smiling she said, "Stop creating a chaos out of nothing. Adil please leave, thanks for the coffee. And you Chandu ji, what have we come here for? For Adil or Adrija?"

"Adrija of course," said Chandu in an irked tone.

"Let go and listen," replied Naina.

Adil walked a short distance and suddenly stopped. He took a turn, came near the table and purposely with an intent to interrupt said, "Madam would you like to try some sandwiches. We make really good ones. I assure you to not disappoint and if we fail, do not pay for the same."

Chandu got pissed to another level and screamed, "Do one thing, get a chair and sit next to us. Why another chair, rather sit on my head. Come. Join us. Come-come sit on my head." With this Chandu got up and held Adil's hand. He literally pulled Adil with much force and insisted upon sitting on his head.

All eyes had turned toward Chandu's table and witnessed the scene. Adil had accomplished the mission of irritating Chandu and getting his hand out, left running to the ordering counter.

With this Chandu sat and told Naina, "Please continue. No more coffee's and sugar sachets please," yelled Chandu from his seat, warning Adil standing at the ordering counter.

"Then what. She shared every bit of information from her past and everything she went through," continued Naina.

"And that is it? This is not enough and offers no help to my case. I want to know about her earlier life and everything that she went through. I know you know, come on without wasting my time, shoot," said a curious Chandu. Although he had no idea of Naina knowing anything about the past, he just took a chance with an aimless claim.

"I cannot reveal what exchanged between us. I have made a pinky promise to Adrija," said Naina.

Chandu appeared baffled on hearing about her 'pinky-promise'. The chance taken by Chandu had hit bulls-eye and he could sense Naina knowing something extra about the past that could help the case. But she appeared reluctant. Losing his calm and banging the table hard he said, "Look miss I am not here for some pinkies and blues, I have come to investigate a serious case. You better speak or I shall make your father turn red out of anger by telling him about your "Dheeraj". And better not take me for granted, it's a pinky promise I will tell your dad."

Naina went pale on hearing the warning, rather it more of sounded like a threat and said, "To know more we will have to go some twelve years back in time."

"So go, what are you waiting for? For some time-machine to get invented and take you in the past? That's not going to happen, so continue," replied Chandu in a stern baritone.

"OK" replied Naina.

"But also let me tell you, I am going to share things that have been shared by Adrija. I don't know how much of it is a fact and how much of it, a cooked story. And yes please don't disclose my name, as in I gave you this information," said an under-confident Naina.

"Please stop engaging me in unwanted things and begin," said Chandu also turning on a recorder (to record all that Naina was about to speak).

12 YEARS AGO

A SNEAK – PEEK IN ADRIJA'S PAST LIFE, TO UNDERSTAND THE PRESENT

CHAPTER 8

THE WORLD CUP NIGHT STORY

2ND APRIL, 2011. Live commentary from the iconic WANKHEDE Stadium, MUMBAI.

"The atmosphere is electrifying and the vibes are nerve-wracking, here at Wankhede stadium, Mumbai. The sub-continent combat, where both the Asian Countries have come a long way, surprising the spectators worldwide. It is the innings break in the Blue v/s Blue final, and one can rightly call this as the clash of the best of the Blues. The stadium appears like an ocean, having every single spectator put on blue t-shirts supporting either of the teams.

Besides the stadium setting, if we talk of those watching from home, streets, sports bar, colleges or wherever TV sets or Projector-screens are setup, the sentiment is the same. Nobody wants to move and wish to stay glued be it whatever, till the very end.

The first half just got over and the crowd is up on their feet. We could have stopped the Lankan Lions at a little less of a score, but the greats that always stand up on any significant day, were no different today. The likes of Sangakara, Jayawardena held their nerves, kept their calm and did what they are best at. They added to a score which psychologically will add some pressure on the Indian team.

The Wankhede pitch is made of red-soil that usually has a

characteristic of behaving uncertainly and mind you it was no different today. And this is what led to the trouble for the Sri Lankan top-order. The pitch played deceptive and did the trick for Indian bowlers. The wickets tumbling at the start, gave Indian bowlers some hope of finishing things early. But as usual the middle order was in no mood to throw away and give up this easily.

Though Kumar Sangakara missed out on a crucial half century, but the captain's contribution of 48 runs from 67 balls anchored the Lankan innings and from there on got the boat sailing. He surely displayed his mettle and led from the front on the day that mattered the most.

Next up to follow and raise the bar for the Lankan side was none other than the deputy himself-Mahela Jayawardene. He surely played the innings of his lifetime. This one will be engraved on his memories for many years to come. Mind you it may turn memorable if Lankans get back home with the WORLD CUP.

The MILESTONE (century) under such pressure, in front of the Indian crowd and on such difficult red-soil 22 yard-stick, has kept the Lankans in hunt. Not only in the hunt but they have posed a target which on any other day might not seem that big, but today being the FINAL- it is no less than a MAMMOTH! The chances are 50-50, fair and square.

Well what has happened cannot be un-done or changed; but what is coming up next, is what we all as Indian fans are looking forward to. Indian conditions, home crowd, home ground of the God of Cricket —Mr. Sachin Tendular, a perfect blend of the experienced batters in the likes of -Sachin, Sehwag and Gambhir and the fearless young blazing pool of talent —Virat, Raina, Yuvraj and Dhoni. Phew, we could not have asked for any better. Moreover, as per the analysts, they believe this is one of the finest Indian side and most competitive to raise the Cup.

Well we are nearing the innings break, just five minutes away from the live action.

Here we go, the master-blaster Sachin, the unapologetic and the ruthless Sehwag- the two Indian openers and one of the successful pairs (as an opening duo) making their way to the field. Both Indian openers look in to the sky as they walk towards the pitch. Maybe they are praying and even thanking God for this opportunity.

Meanwhile, we also see the Sri Lankan unit getting down on the ground- all charged-up and creating an aura around them, of no less than that of the invincible. They appear all poised and high on confidence.

The man with the golden arm and with the most deceptive bowling action in the cricketing world- Lasith Malinga has the new ball in hands.

So one last time we will see the two teams combating for the Cup. We all are ready, the atmosphere is set, the umpires are ready. The umpire signals PLAY!

It will be Sehwag v/s Malinga and here we go.

First ball outside off, Sehwag punches through the covers in full force but well fielded.

Second ball and **OUT!**

Sehwag goes on a duck and the crowd, in absolute shock. This is unbelievable and nothing less than a setback for over 100 crore spectators," the commentary continues on the television set on one hand.

Whereas on the other end (somewhere in Bihar)-

"What the hell was the need for him to be aggressive. He could have waited for a while, deep in the crease and then let himself loose on a bad delivery," said Piyush Jha (PJ) seated in front of the TV at his residence.

"You will comment from here and there, the entire team will listen and implement. What non-sense! Just shut-up and have tea. Do not raise your blood pressure for nothing," replied his wife Kaavya from kitchen, while washing vessels.

"I know that, but it is an emotion. And let me tell you, when every Indian will feel the same and pray for the win, the energy for sure will reach the team. It works, but you will fail to understand the power of vibes," replied Piyush with utmost positivity.

"Oh yes! The balloon of vibes will fly from here and every corner for that matter and reach Mumbai. What the hell are you speaking PJ? You cannot be superstitious just because our team is in the finals. Not to forget then, the vibes of the Lankan fans would be higher (at this juncture of the match) and stronger as compared to us. In any which ways we lie under," replied Kaavya out of sarcasm.

Piyush ignored the answer from Kaavya and set his eyes on the TV screen (once again).

LIVE VISUALS & COMMENTARY FROM THE TV SCREEN-

Just after the jeopardy, an ever-composed, one of the most intellectual batter- Gautam Gambhir, comes to the center. He takes guard and prepares himself to face the first delivery.

Malinga being high on confidence comes beaming for the next delivery and targets the pads. Gambhir with his usual calmness, effortlessly directs the ball to the leg-side boundary.

Seeing this, on one side where Malinga gives a cheeky smile to the batter, Gambhir on the flip side, appeared expressionless.

Coming back to Piyush's residence-

Piyush revives smile on seeing the boundary and says, "Look I told you about the positive vibes. You just manage (what you are good at) your kitchen and stop commenting on the cricket part. Make something really nice."

As the mood sets going and the innings develop, PJ yells from the couch, "Do one thing make onion and potato fritters to eat". PJ appears all pumped up and in no mood to hear anything against the team.

"Be it any occasion, I am going to be in kitchen only. If he has so much positivity, then why not use it for our relationship rather than those 11 men on TV. Chuck it! No point complaining. Let's deep fry veggies for him, else he will go mad at me," murmurs Kaavya in the kitchen, soaked in absolute irritation.

After a little while, PJ all of a sudden roars, "Yes. Hit that pacer for more boundaries (referring to the bowler). C'mon Sachin your masterclass, I want a century from you today."

"He is no Kaavya (to oblige) and nor is he listening to you. Forget the boundaries and get yourselves settled. I am getting delicious fritters in 10 minutes," replied Kaavya from the kitchen, trying to reduce the tension in the atmosphere.

"Concentrate on your job and do not try to be an expert at everything," replied Piyush with utmost displeasure. The tenor in which he threw tantrum was no less than a warning for Kaavya (indirectly). Piyush seemed unstoppable and did not wish to calm down.

Soon with this, the masterclass hit another boundary and Piyush literally jumped off the couch, pumping the air with delight. His happiness knew no bounds, nor did he wish to tame his flurry of emotions.

Kaavya witnessed it all and praying to the God she murmured to self, "I hope the guy (Sachin) continues to hit boundaries and doesn't stop. Or else it will be difficult to handle my man and impossible to stop him from going nuts."

Ten minutes after (as said by Kaavya), she was ready with the fritters and put it to a plate. Kaavya garnished the dish with some fresh coriander leaves and made a smiley (with Ketchup) at the bottom of the plate. As Kaavya stepped out of the kitchen with the dish in her hands and smile on the face, she overheared Piyush shouting, "What the FUCK!"

Kaavya rushed to the sitting area, kept the dish on the center table and worried she asked, "Is everything alright? What happened?"

Piyush seated in shock. On seeing Kaavya said, "Why the hell did you get out of the kitchen? Look what have you done. Sachin is walking back to the pavilion. You bloody curse of a woman."

Kaavya was moved by use of such language and appeared disturbed. However, as she turned towards TV, Kaavya witnessed

(THE VISUALS ON THE TV SCREEN)-

Sachin leaving the ground. Dejected by the shot selection, the master knew he had done a big mistake. As he walked back, not even once did he raise his head and dared to look at the disappointed crowd.

It was this man Malinga again, doing wonders for the Sri Lankan team and it is his DELIVERY that silenced a BILLION. Just when the Indian dug-out and the entire country tried to recuperate, another shocker overshadowed on the hopes of the entire nation.

Absolute silence encapsulated the space of Wankhede and the hope of every Indian of getting their hands on the CUP tonight, began to diminish. There was rage, a feeling of numbness, terror and a bag of mixed emotions everywhere.

At Piyush's residence-

Piyush appeared no different and went through the same sentiments. Deviating from the ongoing scenario, he looked at Kaavya and ordered, "Get a glass of scotch for me, I need to come out of this trauma. If you would have not come out, this would have not happened."

Kaavya stood still near the center table. This further agitated Piyush and raising his voice to the maximum, Piyush repeated, "GO and get a glass of drink. Do not fucking stand on my head."

Kaavya felt disrespected and all frantic she replied, "Are you insane? Me getting out of the kitchen, has got the man out? Are you kidding me? Stop being superstitious. I am not getting you anything. Get up and get it yourself."

Piyush could not withstand the reply from Kaavya. In no time he got up, held Kaavya through hands and vehemently dragged her to kitchen. Kaavya resisted and tried hard, but failed in front of the force.

Finally, as they reached the kitchen entrance, Piyush gave a final push to Kaavya and locking the door from outside said, "Stay in. This is where you belong and you should not try coming out, especially at these crucial times. Enjoy."

Kaavya was filled with fury and weeping she yelled from inside, "You got to pay for this. Dare you also move to eat, drink, loo or for anything for that matter. Just get your ass glued in front of TV and do not move till this match is done."

To this Piyush replied (loud enough to pass through the locked door) with a wicked smile, "Thanks for the advice but mind your own business and do not interfere with mine. Just put something in your mouth, that would help you to shut-up."

With this Piyush engaged himself back with the match.

Live visuals from the cricket ground-

The on-going celebrations in the Lankan dug-out and their fans, had irked Piyush as well as every Indian supporter furhter. On one hand where every Indian team supporter looked bloodthirsty, on the other they failed to find a way out of the hardship.

Five hours or so back then, what appeared like a dream of being into the final, suddenly turned into a sensation of no less than a nightmare. Few also felt the current scenario being a replica of the 2003 World Cup final against Australia. The entire Indian line-up (in 2003) chasing the target, succumbed to the pressure without even giving it a try (as quoted by the experts back then). And result- was a loss in the finals.

The eyes turned moist, the thumping began to weaken and the hopes blundered. Amid all this, we could see the very young, very talented and the chase enthusiast- Virat kohli taking guard on the pitch.

On witnessing the experienced tumbling in front of the lethal bowling attack, Piyush and every other Indian fan had very little or no hopes from the youngster.

For the next three overs or so, the Indian batters were pushed on the back-foot. Their innings appeared jittery and it was very much evident, as they just tried to protect their wickets. However, post those setbacks, the Gambhir-Kohli duo (co-incidentally both from Delhi) tried to anchor the innings.

DRINKS BREAK...

Coming back to Jha residence-

Piyush continued to drink and Kaavya suffered inside kitchen. Fans or spectators turning superstitious is not new and does not come as a surprise, especially on occasions like these; but the extent to which Piyush went was unacceptable. Moreover, he had no regrets and continued his entertainment without feeling of what Kaavya must be going through.

MATCH RESUMES. BACK TO LIVE ACTION...

After a lot of hard-work and caution, the team total reached to 100 in 20th over. This felt like some respite and the momentum got going. Just when the smiles had returned on faces, the fans faced another jolt. Dilshan had applied breaks to the speeding Gambhir-Kohli partnership, by picking up latter's wicket.

Trust me even Dilshan had not imagined of pulling off such a blinder. Kohli had timed the ball sweetly and expected it to go past the non-striker. However, Dilshan managed to put his hand in the air and the leather sphere (by fluke) got stuck in his hands. Kohli and those being on team India side, could hardly believe their luck. But no matter what, he had to leave the ground.

The crowd that kept going and chanted INDIA, INDIAAA.... INDIA, INDIAAA.., had been silenced yet again. This made the entire crowd speechless and mum.

Piyush at his home was sitting and enjoying his drink-

Seeing Kohli depart, Piyush threw the TV remote (held in his hand) hard. The remote crumbled to pieces, such being the intensity. Soon after, he got up from the couch, coming close to the screen (almost less than a feet) said, "What the hell are you guys doing? Today is the only chance to win the cup. If not today, then forget for another three decades or so. Best team, home ground and local supporters, still you guys are ruining the event."

Piyush and many others turned restless, rather most of them. It was still a task to achieve for the Indian team, as they required 161 off 170 balls.

All of a sudden the entire Indian fan fraternity witnessed the unexpected. They saw the man with JERSEY NO. 7 putting his gloves and cap on, getting down the dressing room. **DHONI** it is! The man had promoted himself ahead of the in-form Yuvraj Singh, that too on a final night.

Dhoni always assessed the situation and came on field with a plan. Surely, today was no different. The time he entered the ground, most of the spectators began chanting "Dhoni, Dhoni. Dhoni…. Dhoni." And the entire stadium resonated with Dhoni's name.

However, there were even few like Piyush who were upset with his decision. Piyush on seeing the captain taking guard, started talking to the TV screen, "Haiiiiii…. Dhoni bhaiya (brother)? Why the hell Yuvi has not come to bat? Dhoni-bhaiya, I agree, you got us the debut (20-20) world cup, we get it, but putting yourself ahead in these crucial times is no good decision. Please send Yuvi," said Piyush getting down on his knees with folded hands and pleading.

Piyush had gone bonkers and lost sense. He was high on drinks and seemed like drooling over the screen. He was hoping the Indian cricket ODI team captain to over-turn his decision. His expectations were high for sure, but at the same time vague. This was total display of insanity.

There were many against his decision (even those who usually are the supporters in any other given situation). But, Dhoni being himself, there is nothing that the man did without any reason. Even in this tricky situation he came down on field as cool as a cucumber and with his usual calmness.

VISUALS FORM THE GROUND-

Not bothering much about the situation, Dhoni started in his typical style- defending a few deliveries and trying to understand the nature of the pitch. He created a comfort space for himself for a few upcoming deliveries and did what he is best known for- running between the wickets. This kept the scoreboard ticking and the pressure (after Dhoni's entry) never mounted on the Indian side.

The innings began to build; nevertheless, bad deliveries were hit for boundaries. Thus, Indian batters kept the asking run-rate in control. Proving himself correct, Dhoni went on seamlessly and in no time he achieved a feat on the night of the finals- his maiden half century of the tournament.

Same Piyush (back home) who wanted Dhoni to go back and send Yuvi, seeing Dhoni reach 50, said, "Waah, Dhoni bhaiya. 50. Waah. I knew you would hold on your heads high and it is your geniuses that can take our team home. Very good, do not stop and keep going." Piyush changed his side like a chameleon and surprisingly there were many others like him.

At one point it was Gambhir soaking all the pressure. But, after Dhoni's arrival, the pressure got released and Gambhir played the perfect supporting aid to the master. Dhoni took maximum strike and his hunger to not let this stop in between, rather taking his side (from here on) home, with a CUP, was evident in his character.

Second delivery of the 42nd over.

It is Gambhir v/s Thisara Perera.

And it was a heart-break moment for many. Especially, for

the man - the Great Gambhir, who remained calmest and most focused on the night of this epic battle. The batsman against all odds and with great acumen of the pitch, got India this close to win selflessly and unfortunately got **OUT**.

Yes, Gambhir was cleaned up by Perera on 97 and he missed a century on the final night. On the more when it seemed India were on the winning side. Entire country felt bad on him missing out on century but the hopes stayed afloat, because Mr. Dhoni was still present at the center.

"You hurried a bit, hence punished. There was no need for you to come down the track and play a slog shot. You could afford to waste a delivery or two, especially when Dhoni-bhaiya was at the non-striker's end. Well its ok and well-played. You are going back after playing your role as an anchor and should go with sense of pride," commented Piyush sitting back at home, comfortably in front of his screen. He was high and hardly realized that his opinion did not matter, nor did his comment of appreciation reached Gambhir.

But in the end well-played Gambhir. Although, Perera had sent back Gambhir, the entire Lankan unit refrained themselves from any sort of celebration. Maybe, because they knew the flamboyance and swag of the upcoming batter.

Yes, with this departure came the in-form and the most wanted batter of the night- Yuvraj Singh to the crease. And as expected Yuvi ended the over with a boundary.

Finally, it was 48 runs needed from 48 deliveries.

The run-rate had come down to run-a-ball and by the look of in-form Indian batters it appeared a cake-walk. From here on, there was something that changed and Dhoni shifted gears. From being a serene him, he went full throttle and started hitting the ball for boundaries.

Soon, Yuvi joined the party and it was a two way attack that Lankan team faced. It appeared as if the duo was competing for runs amongst themselves.

And finally, after the 48th over, the scoreboard showed 270 for the loss of 4 wickets.

It was five needed of the twelve deliveries.

Piyush who remained glued to the screen (at a mere distance of less than a feet) said, "I should have come and sat here before. Since the time I have come here, look at India marching with comfort. Silly me. C'mon India. India… India… India… Kaavya see India is about to win. Kaaavayaaa… Love you Kaavya," a high on drinks Piyush continued.

Kaavya did not even respond and it was not known what had happened to Kaavya.

Coming back to the match, on strike Yuvi took a single on the first ball of 49th over. And this got the man of the moment- Dhoni on strike. As Kulasekara came up with his second delivery-

SIX…. DHONI FINISHES OFF IN STYLE.

Dhoni whipped and steered the ball out of the park. He could not believe the moment. What a way to get the curtains down on the night of the final. The Indian dressing room, the entire stadium, the streets and every individual at every corner of the nation erupted out of joy. India is a WORLD CHAMPION, yet again after 28 years.

Meanwhile at Piyush's residence-

Piyush sobbed out of joy. He was unable to sink in the feeling. Piyush lied flat on the floor, looking at the TV he said, "This will be one of those moments I will remember, till I die. Thank you team INDIA."

As the celebrations continued on TV and entire India, Piyush recollected of Kaavya being locked. He got up, opened the lock, saw Kaavya sleeping on the floor. Waking her up, Piyush shared, "Kaavya India won. See, in a way, your locking up paid off. Now you cannot complaint of this being without a reason."

Kaavya had her eyes red out of anger. She did not respond. Rather got up, pushed Piyush out of the way and went to the dining room.

"Kaavya listen naa, let's celebrate. We are the champions. Hey, Kaavya please darling listen naa. Kaavya," Piyush kept calling her from behind but she did not stop.

Kaavya went near the table which had empty bottles and as Piyush approached Kaavya from behind- BANG! Kaavya broke the scotch bottle on Piyush's head.

Piyush felt flat instantly and his head bled badly. In no time, there was blood all over the dining area. Kaavya held Piyush through his collar and said, "Dare you push or ill-treat me ever again," and she pushed Piyush back. Piyush tried to speak but before he could utter, he died (possibly due to excessive bleeding and hemorrhage).

Kaavya went near the body lying in the pool of blood and said, "Piyush, Piyush. Freak he is dead. Piyush," she kept calling him but he did not respond. Kaavya panicked and did not know what to do. She apologized to his dead body and tried cleaning the scene.

As Piyush quoted he would remember the win till his last breath, he did so very much. But the only thing Piyush did not know, that he would breathe his last within 30 minutes of this statement. The night where entire country celebrated the win, Kaavya mourned his husband's death. Albeit, Kaavya herself was responsible, for the same.

PRESENT DAY- CONVERSATION BETWEEN NAINA & CHANDU CONTNIUES -

"This is what Adrija told me about that night. She witnessed the entire episode standing behind a structure and went in shock. Moreover, her mother smartly cleaned up everything and told the visitors (who came to offer condolences) that- Piyush died as he slipped due to wet floor," said Naina describing the incident in detail.

"What about her mother? How did she die?" asked Chandu.

Naina made faces and was reluctant on speaking. However, on seeing Chandu turning furious she said, "Adrija killed her."

"WHAT!," bawled Chandu out of shock.

"Yes, I too was unable to digest but this is what she told me one day. I remember very well, it was her father's 6th death anniversary on 2nd April 2017, when she sat all alone in a corner. When I asked the reason for the same, it was the day she told me the above story of that World Cup night. The inner me was shattered to pieces and broken totally. I could not even imagine what Adrija went through that night or she felt while recollecting the incident," replied Naina.

"I am not interested in knowing what and how she told you about those incidents. Just tell me about her mother's death," an extremely curious Chandu asked.

"Coming to that, wait. This is even more horrifying and gruesome. As she finished talking about her dad, she did not stop and continued-

DIWALI 2012-

One of the most loved festivals of India- Diwali. A beautiful night- with illuminations, candles, rangolis, decorations and firecrackers all around. It is celebrated like a huge carnival and beyond. It is almost like a month-long festival; the celebrations begin a fortnight before and continue till a week later. There are smiles, joys, greetings, love, and warmth exchanged all around.

Tuesday 13th November, 2012- Diwali Night.

This day was no different and the entire city was lit up, decorated and there was cheerfulness all around in the air. Adrija along with her mom was on the streets just outside her house, enjoying the evening. The sky dazzled with different types and colors of firecrackers. Everyone contemplated and enjoyed the artificial luminosity that had left the atmosphere shining.

All was well until; Adrija saw a small girl (roughly of her age) turning with her dad. She saw this little girl playing with her dad, sharing jokes, giggling around, and enjoying the fiesta. This made Adrija emotional and she desperately missed having her dad around. Her mom was busy with other friends of the locality, hence missed on noticing Adrja's emotions.

Adrija felt helpless and did not know on how to deal with this hollow sensation. She continued to gaze (the daughter-father duo) from a corner of the street, when suddenly an aerial firecracker caught her eye. Once burnt, these aerial crackers propelled a series of aerial shells and comets; and produced various colors, noises, and wonderful sparkling effect. The best part of these crackers being the shower effect that they created in the sky.

Adrija saw a man having these firecrackers in bulk, so much so that it felt as if he bought one entire shop of those selling the crackers. Adrija got up, quietly went near the heap of these crackers, and stood. She continued to stand for a while and appeared as if she waited for something. Soon, as the man went to burn another cracker, Adrija stole one from the mass and ran back to her position on the street.

On getting back to where she sat, Adrija kept the stolen cracker right in front of her eyes. Her eyes at one moment looked at the cracker and the next instance it stared her mother. This game of eyeballing continued for a while.

After few minutes of thinking, Adrija got up, held the firecracker, and went near her mother. As she stood very close, Adrija saw her mother chuckling and noticed her having a gala time with her associates. Adrija appeared disturbed and something bothered her, for sure. Her mother being so involved in the group, that she failed to spot her daughter, that stood this close.

Adrija stood and observed her mother constantly. After a

while she placed the stolen firecracker at the back of her mother, obviously without her knowledge. Adrija kept the cracker in the horizontal position (usually placed in vertical position) with the opening of the firecracker facing the back of her mother. She had no second thoughts and without any hiccup lit the cracker.

As the rope burnt and reached closer to the gunpowder encapsulated in the cracker, memories of that terrifying night- the night her father died (rather was killed) pondered in Adrija's head. Her eyes were red out of anger and she kept looking venomously at Kaavya, who was still busy sharing light moments with her friends and totally missed on attending Adrija.

After ticking for a few seconds, the burning rope contacted the gunpowder in the cracker and **BOOM**!

The cracker targeted at Kaavya had launched successfully. She was caught up in the flames in seconds. And, soon she started to scream out of pain. The shots went on bursting one after the other and the situation continued to worsen. The circumstance had created chaos all over with the cries of, "Help, Help. Please help Kaavya, she is burning," from everyone.

A lady from Kaavya's friend group, took Adrija in her arms and tried closing her eyes; but Adrija wanted to witness Kaavya's pain, agony, and the suffering all by herself. The little girl had her eyes on the tragedy and saw the incident unfolding but felt nothing. She had turned cold-hearted, rather appeared sadist.

Kaavya kept howling but nobody offered any help. As the cracker went silent Kaavya fell on the streets, unconscious. She suffered more than ninety percent of the burns. The state in which she lied was unthinkable and unimaginable. The crowd around, were horrified by her burnt appearance and none could withstand the sight. Even those friends that giggled with Kaavya prior to the incidence, resisted from offering any help.

Kaavya was slowly losing her breath, while Adrija in her heart was gaining pleasure. Adrija saw it all through the meshed nets of the chiffon saree of Kaavya's friend. As others (from all the on-lookers) wished somebody turning for help, Adrija prayed for her mother's death. Kaavya struggled and fought for her life for over thirty minutes, but none offered any assistance. Finally, Kaavya succumbed to the injuries and Adrija had her revenge complete. THE END"

PRESENT DAY-

After hearing everything that Naina told, Chandu was left flabbergasted. He had gone numb and was unable to sink in the feeling. The vicious side of Adrija at such a tender age had left Chandu shocked.

"Chandu Ji," said Naina.

Chandu did not respond.

Naina nudged again, "Chandu Ji. You fine?"

Chandu finally came out of the shocker, drank a glass of water and as he tried to speak, words failed to come out. He faced difficulty, stammered while speaking and was unable to express.

Looking at this Naina said, "It is ok Chandu Ji, I can understand. Even I reacted in somewhat similar manner after listening to the story. But it is what it is."

Chandu still tried and finally after some recovery in state of mind, said, "I still wish, this to be a story, but also know deep in my mind this being the reality."

After sighing, he continued, "This is impossible, still I got to believe it being real. I feel pity for Kaavya. Poor lady. But yes, also what she did to Piyush was nevertheless unacceptable. So may be karma it is."

As Chandu went on speaking, Naina heard it all and gave an expression of helplessness. Chandu felt mystified on seeing Naina's face and said, "What? Why are you giving me those looks? Are you not done?"

To this Naina just nodded sideways. On seeing the same, Chandu appeared a bit troubled and accumulating courage asked, "What does that nod mean? Is it hinting at some more trembling stories or it indicates the end of this torturous session?"

"I so wished the former was true. But sadly got to go with the latter part," replied Naina.

On hearing upon Naina's reply, Chandu began to feel depressed and dizzy. He was in no condition to take anymore shudders but had to face them, with no options left. Keeping a stone on his heart, Chandu said, "Go on then. What are we waiting for? Everything that is going to come-up is wrong, so no pointing of waiting for the right time."

Naina on getting the kind of reply from Chandu, said, "Are you sure you want to proceed? I mean, is it this necessary for you to dig her past and that too against your will?"

Chandu dreamt for a while and in his dreams, he saw Rudra and Aazad. He saw them hovering around for truth. Chandu had promised every bit of fact about Adrija and hence could not leave without the same. Moreover, there was also a facet of Chandu, which was dying to prove his ability to those young chaps.

Seeing him unresponsive, Naina said, "I do not think you are in any condition to take anymore setbacks. So let us call for the bill and leave."

"Wait," said Chandu in a strong masculine tone.

"Sit down, I want to hear. And mind you lady, this is my duty. It is about someone's life and death. So, sit and continue," said Chandu.

To this Naina replied, "Okay, but why suddenly so much of stress in the tone. We shall continue and I do not have any problems with that." With his Naina sat.

Chandu ordered another coffee, prepared himself for another jolt, and gestured Naina to get going.

Naina set herself up and said, "Okay so let us go a bit ahead in time and talk about 2015."

CHAPTER 9
PROFESSOR'S PUPPY

PATNA, BIHAR- 2015

A private coaching center-Scholar's Academy, Bihar. The establishment was a celebrated coaching institute. It only catered to 10th standard (Board exams appearing) students in entire Patna and was known for delivering the best with guaranteed results. With 100 percent passing ratio (no failed/ drop-out student), the institute was true to its promise and tagline-Learn from the best and be the BEST. It had been successful in giving (back-to-back) state toppers since a decade and other individual subject toppers.

However, getting in to the institution was no cake walk, as it did not entertain any and every student. It had three major check points, surpassing which could only give an entry-

1.   The student wanting to study in the academy had to be amongst the top 10 ranks from their respective schools. This was- the only reason behind 100 percent passing ratio and guaranteed results. This ignited a few rumormongers to spread a word that- institute was biased and catered only the best from the crowd.

2.   The fees were bomb- two lakh for the academic year. Being amongst the best students was not enough, the parents also had to be from the cream section of the society and have a hefty bank

balance. Ironically, the fees were much higher than the cumulative fees of all the government schools in entire Patna.

3.   Not only the students and the bank balance, the third most and weirdest condition of all was- one of the parents (at least) needed to be a graduate from English medium. The ideology behind this being- only then these parents would be able to understand the immense grinding of the students and not consider the process pressurizing the child. Also, the work sheets provided by the academy for practice were next level and beyond imagination.

These were the conditions to get oneself in the academy and compulsorily all boxes needed to tick right.

Adrija studied in Patna Public School and was the brightest student of her class. She always topped in all her academic exams. Along with, Adrija was great at extra-curricular activities and participated in every event held in her school. Being an extra-ordinary student, she was every teacher's favorite and no less than ideal candidate of what would be called as an all-rounder.

Moreover, Adrija came from an above middle-class background. All these factors cumulatively made her eligibility strongest for approaching Scholar's academy. Looking at her career graph, the academy was amazed and without any doubt wanted Adrija on board. Hence, selected on merit.

Professor Anand Kumar-

Being every teacher's first choice, Adrija was dear to every professor at the institute, and especially very close to science professor and the founder of Scholar's Academy -Anand Kumar.

Anand Kumar- the science prodigy Kumar, as he was called by everyone in entire Patna. He was way ahead of his time than the others during his educational days. In a backdrop and the soil known to produce the best of officers; A land where every individual aimed and prepared themselves for Civil Services (mainly IAS & IPS), Anand had different dreams and so wished to be atypical.

In April 1998, when he just cleared class ninth (9) and enjoyed his summer vacations, Anand Kumar had no whereabouts of what to do with his life. What Anand only knew was- he did not wish to join the rat race and emerge as yet another officer (with due respect). But beyond this clarity of not going for civil services, Anand had no goal or aim of how to move ahead or choose something as his future.

A month later (MAY-1998), Anand's life took a major turn and magic happened. 11 to 13th May 1998- an era written with gold in the history of Indian science. A phase which made entire India evident & noticeable on the world maps, all thanks to the science pioneers. The time when nuclear operation **SHAKTI** happened- one fusion and four fission explosions at Pokhran, Rajasthan were carried successfully.

Soon, after the successful tests, Prime Minister Shri Atal Bihari Vajpayee ji announced the very day- India as the full-fledged nuclear state. The operation took place under the leadership of eminent scientists – Dr. APJ Abdul Kalam (chief scientist advisor and director of Defence Research and Development Organisation) and Dr. R. Chidambram (the director of Department of Atomic Energy).

It was a moment of pride for the entire homeland and inspired many young minds to be the next Kalams, Chidambrams, Homi Bhabhas, Vikram Sarabhais and many such great science forerunners. The same incident touched Anand Kumar's heart and he was the one amongst many to be moved by this achievement.

The time the news spread nationwide like fire, was the very day Anand decided to be the next scientist. And, from the very moment he started imagining himself as one of those from ISRO (Indian Space Research Organization). Anand not only dreamt but made sure he worked hard and excelled with flying colors in all he did from- clearing his Boards (10th exams) with distinction to topping the university in high school (12th exams).

Being from a middle-class family, Anand's economic background was not that great, but somehow his parents managed to get him admitted to a decent degree college. By the time Anand got graduated, he absorbed the financial condition of his family. And 2005 was the year- Scholar's Academy took birth. By the way, Anand again topped the university and emerged as the best in Bachelors of Computer Engineering.

It (Scholar's Academy) all started from one room (where his entire family stayed) with 10 students. Passionate about studies, Anand aimed at passing his study techniques to aspiring students (those who had hunger in any field and aimed at nothing less than perfection) and in turn kept polishing his knowledge. Even at the inception, Anand had the same mindset of coaching only those school goers who held top grades.

Undoubtedly, Anand was a great tutor and had immense knowledge with regards to any subject. With the positive word of mouth publicity, the students kept increasing and the monetary condition got better and better, enough to fund his own institutional fees; plus, he emerged as a helping hand at home. 2009 was the year he completed his PhD in Astronomy and was this close to see his dream getting fulfilled.

Anand did it all and sent an application to ISRO. But as it is said- one cannot get greater than what is written in destiny, Anand's case was a classic example. The day Anand received an offer letter from ISRO, was the day he lost his dad and his dream crushed to pieces. He was sitting next to his dad's body (lying on the floor, covered with a white sheet), when post-man came and handed over a letter to Anand.

Survived by a mother and two younger siblings- a brother and smallest a sister, Anand had no other option but chose to stay back in village and be the bread owner for his remaining family. Anand continued to be the professor and expanded his coaching institution, taking it to a perfect commercial stage.

Anand hired more professors, made rules for admissions, himself never stopped learning and teaching. He saw his goal losing but always remained unruffled. Anand was an introvert and possibly the reason of him being lonely, but well settled. Anand not only did good but got his siblings permanently settled in lives. Furthermore, got them wedded with one of the best girl and guy in town, respectively.

In 2015, he was 32 years old. The year when Adrija entered Scholar's Academy. Adrija was attractive even then. Atypical curly hair (very unusual in those times), fair, slim, good stature. Plus, not to forget the wonders she did in academics and beyond. Her speaking skills were no less than amazing and was fluent in every language she spoke. In short, she was a complete package of talent that anyone could imagine; and yet very down to earth.

Adrija was from the ordinary like other girls, yet extra-ordinary. Which meant- neither she came from a very elite society nor she had classy standards. Still, Adrija had a spark to stand out from the crowd and get all eye-balls rolled.

One fine day during a regular class test-

Being an important step in deciding an individual's career, appearing for board exams is never easy. Moreover, at Scholar's Academy the students were literally bombarded with knowledge and grilled with regular mock tests.

This day being one of those from the regular test phases, a strength of 20 students had appeared for the examination. Anand himself was supervising the class-room. All were engrossed and engaged in solving the question paper, when suddenly Anand's phone rang. The phone looked important to Anand, hence in the middle of the tests he said, "Excuse me class, I need to attend this call and shall be right back soon. Until then no discussing and/or cheating. Is that understood?"

"Yes sir," collectively responded the students present.

However, Anand was not sure of leaving the class without

scrutiny. Hence, just before departure Anand gestured, "Adrija come here," who was sitting on the bench, right in front of his table.

"Sir me?" asked Adrija apprehensively.

"Yes, Adrija please come," requested Anand.

Frightened, she got up and as she begun to walk, "Wait. Get your paper and writing material along," said Anand.

Adrija took her answer sheet and pen, as instructed, and walked towards the table. On reaching upon Anand's table, afraid she asked, "Yes sir. What happened? Did I make some mistake?"

"Absolutely not. You are one of the brightest and my most favorite student. So please do not be scared and sit here," said Anand offering the professors seat.

"Sir here? Are you sure? But why?" asked Adrija getting further nervous.

"Please do not hesitate and have a seat. I want you to keep an eye on the class till the time I am back. Be blunt, be unapologetic, but make sure nobody does anything unethical" said Anand and he left with this.

Adrija was shocked and did not expect this appointment. On one hand she was startled and continued writing her tests; on the other- the entire class found it suspicious. The class had thoughts running in their mind and felt something beyond professional. Not thinking about the situation much at the very moment, the class continued with the tests.

15 minutes later, Anand returned to the class room, "Thanks Adrija for the help. Is everything alright?" asked Anand.

Immediately, getting up from the seat, Adrija replied, "Yes sir."

"Good thank you. You may get back to your seat," said Anand Kumar patting on her back.

With this Adrija returned to her seat and continued writing. After an hour the tests got completed and the students left.

At the outside of the academy, just 500 meters away, at one corner of the road, was a famous Xerox shop- Mahadev Xerox and Printers. This xerox center was the assembly point for all students (post every test) to discuss the question paper and estimate the right and the blunders that individuals did during the test.

Today, being no different, the entire group had associated for discussion, except Adrija. Usually, even she participated in these discussions at any given day, but today after facing an awkward situation during the tests, Adrija decided to skip the meeting.

The decision that Adrija took, just to avoid the embarrassment, rather backlashed at her. As she passed right in front from the assembly point, one amongst the group named as Parth commented, "Look at the girl and her altering attitude on a mere appointment. She appears to be filled with arrogance and ego. I just cannot believe she ignored all of us and left."

While another student named Maitri, added to the previous comment, "Seriously man, this girl is lucky. Anand sir is so cute, but look at her. She looks all artificial and plastic beauty. What allured Anand sir remains as a question to me."

And there were many more comments to follow. None, refrained from taunting. The point of discussion, had become point of verbal assassination. These comments suddenly, led to the issuance of character certificate of the ever-innocent Adrija. She heard it all as she walked-by the xerox center. Although, Adrija pretended unaffected from outside, she had her eyes moist and was deeply hurt inside.

From the day of appointment, something changed from Anand's side and Adrija started receiving more attention. Anand's approach looked more casual with Adrija; and biased as compared to other students.

Slowly and steadily, it was observed that Anand failed to give same kind of importance to other students of the batch; and with time his partial nature became openly evident. This soon became the trending gossip of the entire academy and there was no shutting to these ever-blabbering mouths.

Adrija, began to face more hatred from all the batchmates and there were none who shared an affable relationship with her. Helpless with the given situation, she faced it all silently, tried avoiding all the daily rumors and concentrated on the career.

One fine day-

Outside the academy at the very own Mahadev Xerox center, the entire gang (Adrija's classmates) stood and discussed the question paper of the just given examination. Unexpectedly, a cute brown colored dog (Indian Pariah breed commonly found all over India) with asymmetrical white patches all over, came from behind and stood besides the group.

"How cute! I have been noticing this dog from a long distance, for quite a few days now, but never witnessed this close. The dog looked adorable distantly, but even more cute at this proximity," said Maitri. With this, the momentum from solving the question paper shifted to the recently arrived endearing dog.

"Oh yes indeed! He is charming. It is difficult to give him a miss when this close. Being brown and alluring, how about calling him Brownie? Isn't that apt and suits his personality?" added Shamaa (pointing at the dog), another student from the group. Soon, with this Shamaa got down on her knees, held the dog around his neck and began cuddling.

On hearing upon the name, everyone responded collectively, "Cool name- Brownie. Yes, Brownie, Brownie…". The entire group appeared happy and pleased. The group made a circle with Brownie at the center and pampered the breed.

All was well and joyous, when suddenly the batch saw a small pup approaching Brownie. As the pup neared, Keshav (another batchmate) appeared confused and said, "Hey! The pup belongs to Brownie? Seriously? I doubt and the not so appealing character of the pup, validates the same."

Turning her eyes at the incoming pup, Maitri added, "Oh yes you are right. Also, this reminds me of the bond between Anand sir and Adrija. Our professor being so handsome and dashing, whereas Adrija…. Yakkk… absolutely not. It feels nauseating when I see them together."

With this, everybody laughed and laughed out loud. In the middle of the light-hearted moment, Parth added, "C'mon Maitri you cannot be mean. You cannot compare the little one (pup) with Adrija. It is so disgraceful to the pup." And there was a laugh riot and everybody went mad giggling.

Continuing in the same pattern, Shamaa added, "Surely this Brownie-pup duo reminds us of Anand-Adrija connection, great observation Maitri. Nevertheless, this also makes me conclude that you are no less than a bitch. You disliked Adrija from the very day Anand Sir started inclining toward her, but today this comparison has made it evident. Also, hinting at next-level of rivalry."

"Ha. Ha. Ha. Call me by any name bitch or witch, but the fact remains unaffected. This pair surely reminds us of those two. From, here on whenever we spot those two together (in the academy) they will always be relatable to this duo," said Maitri in a wicked tone.

While the entire group had their discussions on and everybody commented on the Brownie-pup as well as Anand-Adrija relationship; they stopped the little pup getting close to Brownie. The pup tried every bit to get close to his father, but the students teased the pup by picking him up every time he came closest to Brownie. After a point when pup failed to get close to his father, it cried and continued to do so. But the entire group remained unaffected and enjoyed the torment.

After sharing infinite comments and having a ball for over thirty minutes, Parth prompted, "How about calling Adrija- The Professor's Puppy? Isn't this apt for her guys? Like it sounds so applicable and convincing."

"Freak Parth, what a title! Too good and how creative of you," said Avni immediately and pulled his cheeks. To this Parth blushed and Avni in return gave a mushy smile.

"Thank you Avni, happy you liked it," responded Parth on getting appreciated by his crush and his cheeks went red even further.

"Even we love the name given to Adrija. We also feel like pulling your cheeks out of adoration. Shall we?" teased the two boys from the group with an intent of pulling legs.

Parth showed a punch and replied with a gesture of hitting with the same. Looking at which, the two boys giggled.

"C'mon guys do not shift gears and deviate from the important topic. So, it stands decided that Adrija will now be called by her newly given title- The Professor's Puppy! Is that clear?" asked Maitri with an intent of confirmation.

Obviously, to which entire group agreed and sounded affirmative.

From the very day Adrija was teased by her new name whenever she came across any of her batch mates. It was hurtful and being unable to help herself, was even worse for Adrija. She felt depressed at times, but had no way out. Adrija failed to understand on why she was associated with Anand Sir and often went blank when unable to find any answer.

There was nothing ever Anand hinted at the soft side, nor did Adrija looked in the particular angle. But the entire academy had built this bubble of myth and was assured with something coy between the two. Occasionally, after a while, even Adrija doubted her instincts and felt she missed on observing the indications from Anand Sir's side.

However, being a brilliant career-oriented student, Adrija avoided the ongoing shit and concentrated on her studies. The mockery continued at one end and increased with every passing day; on the flip side it made Adrija more strong and resistant to the on-going travesty. Time flew and the board examination time neared.

GOOD NEWS-

In the atmosphere fueled with tension and apprehensions, a fortnight before the final exams, "Hi all. I hope everyone is prepping and geared-up to enter the ultimate lap. To ease and relax you all a bit, there is a good news for a few of you," announced Professor Amit addressing to the class in an all excited tone.

The class appeared confused and failed to understand on how to react to the announcement; as Amit Sir mentioned it to be a good one only for a handful of students. On one hand where excitement was making its way through the intense environment; on the other entire class appeared bamboozled.

Upon seeing the perplexed faces, Professor Amit continued in the enigmatic manner, "Do not get tensed, there is nothing to lose. But there is something up for the grab for sure."

These jumbled sentences and guess-what type of talks, further escalated the anxiety of the class. Unable to absorb this suspense kind of a scenario, one of the students named Mehmood said, "Sir, please stop behaving like Gulzar sahib, whose lyrics are soothing to the ears but the meaning of the same go from over the head. Please explain the context of the contest like Javed sahib whose writings are rather- pacifying, soothing and understandable at the same time."

To this Amit replied with all zeal and energies, "We, the teaching faculty have collectively come to a decision to take the students for a day outing. That too at the Om Resorts."

As soon as the statement fell on the ear drums, all began to hoot. All pumped up environment had led to disremembering of the nervous part.

Amit interjected soon and said, "Well, this opportunity will only be applicable to top-five apprentices from the academy. So this day outing will be executed once the results are out and we know our scholars."

The entire class went in silence as if taken aback by some shock. Furthermore, Amit added, "So buckle-up class and put the medal on the pedal. It's battle time and for sure worth fighting. So, here's wishing you all- A great luck ahead!"

The contest had made the exams even more interesting and every individual vowed to excel as well as perform better than the rest.

The time passed by and the day of examination arrived. Each and every individual gave beyond 100 percent due to the extra push and motivation received just before the boards. In no time, the tests got over and everyone waited for the results with bated breath.

There were no more classes and no anymore stories/ instances of Anand-Adrija meet-ups. During this period, Adrija missed those little moments- where she hung around Anand sir. On being away from the academy (especially Anand sir) Adrija also felt the lacking of that extra attention. There was a sudden stoppage to everything after the examinations. Plus, she was devoid of any motives to go meet Anand sir in person. The results were scheduled to be declared after a month or so. Hence no relief to Adrija's emotions, anytime soon.

One of the nights in her room, "You know Dad I am very confused. I am unable to sink in this feeling of separation. I had nothing in my heart when I went to class, but this sudden arrival of emotion is out of my handling capacity. When around him, I never felt the urge for anything, or for that matter nothing appeared special. Although, my fellow class mates always hyped and exaggerated about the situation. I am unaware of what is this called? Others call it love, but I do not see any clear signals from his end. Does he also feel for me in similar manner, or is it only me and my over-thinking inner-self that is causing uneasiness. Reply Dad, please. I am in a dilemma and this emotion has overshadowed and numbed the other senses inside." Yes, this was the very first instance where she hallucinated the presence of her departed father.

This was not all, Adrija also in the mind had a reply from her dad. After a while of repetitive budge, she out of the figment of imagination, "Look Adrija do not pay heed to what others have to say, just listen to your heart. World can be manipulative and it can hurt you, but your heart is yours and will never let you down. You do what you feel is right and not what others think is. Got it!" she had this reply (a delusionary one though).

As Adrija finished fantasizing, her maid knocked at the door of the room from outside and said, "Dinner is ready Adrija, come fast. I have made your favorite Paneer handi. Come fast."

"Coming amma," replied Adrija.

"Wow paneer handi! So sorry dad, I am hungry and after listening to my favorite dish, it has become even more difficult to resist. I will catch up with you post dinner. Thank you for the advice," and with this Adrija left the room.

These were the first signs of her mental illness as Adrija hallucinated her dad's presence. Maybe, she was high on emotions after a very long time and the same triggered the very corner of the brain which should not have been hindered.

The month long wait ended and came the day of results. With no surprise and second thoughts, Adrija topped the academy as well as the entire state. Adrija had become the talk of the town. Soon, Adrija received an invitation from the academy on the very day and she obliged in no time.

Anand along with entire staff and other students waited for Adrija's arrival. As soon as Adrija arrived, Anand welcomed her with bouquet of flowers and hugged right after, in front of the entire academy. As Anand continued to hold Adrija in his arms, he said, "Many congratulations on achieving this feat and I am so proud of you. You have wiped-out all past records and scored the highest, ever in the history of this academy. Well done."

The eyes of everybody present (including students and teaching faculty) went in disbelief and had popped out on experiencing the current ongoing warmth exchange program between Anand & Adrija. All that Adrija missed during one month or more, was compensated in this one hug and she felt on top of the world.

Not bothered about the on-lookers for the very first time, even she hugged Anand with equal affection. This course of action in a way made Adrija believe that even Anand had feelings for her and there existed a soft-corner in his heart. Though the duration of the hug would not have lasted over 30 seconds, but these moments were enough to convey Anand's feeling.

Post this, the celebration further continued with cake-cutting and distribution of snacks in the academy. Amidst all this Professor Chaitali said, "As promised, we are all set for the day picnic. We have our top five- Adrija, Shamaa, Parth, Azhar and Max. So heartily Congratulations to all. You have done your part, now stands our chance to fulfil the commitment. We will be leaving for Om Resorts day after, sharp at 7 a.m. Request you five to gather here in the premises prior to the departure. Please do not be late. Till then celebrate the victory and keep enjoying."

With this the party continued and everybody appeared elated.

Same night Adrija's room-

Adrija lied on bed. Gazing at the ceiling fan she kept thinking about all that transpired during the celebration. Adrija was indeed all excited with the kind of affection she received from Anand Sir. This in turn, had also confirmed of Anand having equal and considerable feelings for Adrija (this is what Adrija concluded).

As Adrija continued to ponder and recollected the events, she could sense the incoming of her dad. Yet again, the over-excitement had triggered the wrong region of her brain and with all anticipation she said, "Thank God you are here. I cannot express how happy I am today. You were right dad- about following the inner instinct. Today, Anand sir embraced me with such fondness, that I could feel the intensity and intent."

Her eyes smoldered as she spoke, the vibes made Adrija feel

ecstatic and her cheeks went red as the cupid had struck the chord. She continued blushing, "I am going to express my feelings on the day of outing and cannot wait to hold on to his hands," and Adrija slept with the very enthusiasm.

The calmness, Adrija had on her face while she was asleep, was seen after ages. Probably, the kind of care and attention she received from Anand was the reason behind the same. Also, after her father's death and mother's shocking end, Adrija was all by herself in the years that followed.

Where on one hand, it appeared that happiness waited with open arms to hug Adrija's life and supposedly hinted at only good things to follow; on the other- she imagining her father's presence, hinted at the rise of- what can be called as potential threat to herself or to the society or both.

Adrija had reached a state of delusion and dilemma, where she was unable to distinguish between the real and the unreal. The line between the fact and fantasy appeared to diminish with every passing day in Adrija's case. This in turn meant, increased risk of her returning to actuality and negligence of unforeseen events to take place.

The outing at Om Resorts-

The day arrived. The gang of students Adrija, Shamaa, Parth, Azhar and Max were ready and raring to go. The group reported sharp at 7 a.m at the academy premises. While, the teacher's assemblage having Chailtali, Amit and Anand Kumar himself, joined. Collectively they got in the booked SUV car and left for the resorts.

On their way, the barrier of the student-teacher correlation was not relevant anymore and all acted like friends. They enjoyed every bit while traveling and appeared thrilled on their journey to the resorts.

After covering a distance of more than 100 kilometers and a travel time of hour and a half, the group finally reached their destination. The entrance was densely crowded and there appeared a long queue at the ticket counter. Anand Sir, got in the queue and patiently waited for the turn.

Getting over all the hustle and bustle, Anand finally collected the tickets and they were all set to enter the resorts. Upon entering, the group was fascinated by the entire setting of Om resorts. Prior to this visit, each one had heard a lot of great things about the resort and it was also claimed (by many) as one of its kind in the entire Bihar state, but none had witnessed.

Upon entering, the rumors heard were proven to be true. The resorts were not only distinct in entire Bihar, rather an exclusive one across the nation. It was amongst the few in entire India, to have an amalgamation of water and land rides.

Apart from the land and water extravaganza, it had thrilling adventure sports. The ones that caught attention to the maximum were- rock climbing, zip-line, rappelling, bungee-jumping and trampoline as the major attractions. Even at the look of this entire arrangement, it appeared entrancing enough and gave adrenaline-rush to those who enjoyed these brave-seeking canters. It was the only establishment in the entire state, to have these kind of adventure-seeking escapades. Hence, never short of crowd and everyday there were thousands that visited this resort.

Everything said and done, the one who wished to give all the exciting avenues a miss, could relax in a huge swimming pool at the center of the resort. It was big enough with a depth varying from 3 feet at one end to 15 feet at the other, also having a diving area at the latter end. Adjoining the humongous pool was a tiny little hole with collection of water, for the kids to play; although big enough to be called as a kid's pool. In short, there was everything for everyone visiting the resort.

Not to miss on mentioning, the entire localizing was at shore side of the famous river Ganga. Hence, the resort also had a private access to this beautiful esplanade for all its visitors. Thus, the one visiting this resort who felt like doing absolutely nothing, could spend the me-time at the shore. This beach-side entrance was like an icing on the cake. Phew! There was lot to do at the Om resorts and one could never return with an empty or missed out feeling.

The entire lot of eight members stood confused and pondered over the start point. There was so much to do that none were able to finalize the beginning point of their journey. After pondering for a while, they saw land-slides section having comparatively less rush; hence choosing it as the point of initiation.

From one ride to the other, to another and so on and so forth, they kept hopping and reveled each of these breath-taking rides. The time flew in a jiffy and it was already noon by the time they got done with these terrestrial spectacular. Devoid of energies and tired, the group decided to take a lunch-break. They gobbled on the mouth-watering dishes and revived their bodies for the next set of activities.

Post lunch, everyone felt extremely heavy and full. Unable to move and on exceedingly feeling lazy, the group mutually decided to take some time off from the adventurous journey and relax in the pool, till the time the food settled. However, Anand differed from joining and chose to spend some time by the esplanade.

Barring Mr. Kumar, all went ahead as decided, to spend some time in pool. After laying for a good 45 minutes in water, they geared up themselves for the aquatic spree. However, just before this aqua-journo initiation, Adrija detached herself from the group and wished to not continue anymore. Being unaffected by her decision, rest went on to enjoy.

Adrija had other plans. She took this as an opportunity to approach Anand Sir (who sat all alone at the shore) and convey what she felt. On making up the mind, Adrija went on to change her swimming costume, skidded in her casual attire and soon after she went searching for Anand Sir.

Adrija went searching and kept doing so for over a kilometer but was unable to find Anand Sir. As she neared the dead-end of the beach, her hopes resonated with the end and diminished with every foot forward. However, just before the extreme, she finally saw Anand Sir sitting at the farthest possible extent of the beach. Adrija had a breather and smiled at the glance of Anand Sir. Unable to hold on any longer, she brisk walked towards him.

Immersed in thoughts of his own, Anand sir did nothing, but just gazed at the incoming waves at the shore. He even missed on observing Adrija, who stood at a distance of less than a meter.

Adrija adored looking at this engrossed side of Anand Sir and so did not wish to disturb him; but having a fear of others coming and hindering with privacy, she approached Anand Sir. Impending Adrija said, "Hi sir. I hope I am not intruding your personal space nor am I interfering with your me-time."

The very presence of Adrija had Anand smiling. With the same joyous expression, he replied, "Oh absolutely not. I was enjoying this wonderful landscape of the sun dunking down into the sea, accompanied by the music of these roaring waves hitting the rocks at the shore. The scenario appeared captivating and now with you being besides, the beauty of the setting has just enhanced."

To this Adrija blushed and remained mum.

"How come you are out so soon and not with the group? Are you not having a good time at the resort?" asked Anand casually.

"Certainly, I am having a great time and liking every corner of this wonderland; but enough for the day. I am exhausted and covering the entire fairyland in a day is not my thing. The energies have drained to the extremity, so I rather opted myself out of the association," replied Adrija.

After a short pause she continued, "Additionally, coming here and missing out on this part of the resort was impossible. Therefore,

I decided to detach from all the hustle and spend some time with myself, just like you. I hope you do not mind on me being around you."

"Not at all. The boulevard very much belongs to you, as much as it does to me. After all, we have individually paid for the tickets," said Anand and chuckled. On hearing the comment, even Adrija giggled along.

As the two continued laughing and shared light moments, the sun had dipped in the sea and the moon with full illumination was up in the sky and beaming. The stars around the sphere had spread all across the sky, adding to the feel of this beautiful setting. The landscape appeared dreamy and the environment perfect enough, for expressing what Adrija had arrived for.

Breaking the silence and cutting through the serenity, suddenly, Adrija asked, "Can I ask you something?"

Anand still seeming jovial and easy to connect, replied, "Yes of course. Why something! Ask me anything and everything that you wish to."

This reply elevated Adrija's confidence level and coming straight to the point she asked, "What do you think and feel about me?"

"This is what you took consent for? Seriously! C'mon you need not be seeking permissions for these stupid things. Coming to the answer, you are a wonderful student and undoubtedly, will be having a brilliant future," replied Anand.

To this Adrija instantaneously replied, "I am not talking career-wise. What I mean is, do you like me as a person?"

"Absolutely, who would not like you. You are a wonderful human being, and one of the finest I have ever come across. You have an alluring persona and flamboyance written all over your character," replied Anand with intensity.

Adrija still appeared very much disappointed with the reply she got. Moreover, she was disappointed with herself, on being unable to convey what she meant. Trying to go head on and all out, Adrija directly asked, "Do you feel for me? I mean do you like me?"

Anand felt stupefied. He appeared dazed and enigmatic. Supposedly, he was not expecting this from Adrija. Thus, such a question from her end, had made him uncomfortable. The facial expressions had very well made evident of what Anand felt inside and made Adrija very much nervy.

Still, she was awaiting a verbal dialogue. Anand on the other hand had zipped his lips and uttered nothing. Adrija continued to feel restless and feeling of the same increased, with every passing moment.

After the exchange of all the rugged vibes between the two and waiting for a while, Adrija broke the ice and said, "Sir, I am waiting."

Anand unwillingly, in a sulking tone said, "I do not know the reason behind the rise of such a sentiment and I am still in state of shock after such an advancement. But I will come straight and honest- I have nothing for you nor do I feel in a manner you do. I like your radiating character and you as a sorted individual. That's all about it and nothing beyond."

Adrija appeared broken on hearing the reply. She got the answer and understood every word said by Anand clear and with no hiccups. Yet, Adrija thought of reconfirming once and repeated herself, "Are you sure of not feeling anything beyond this?" As she asked this again, Adrija appeared sinking deep in the sea of displeasure and discontent, yet wished the answer to change. Her emotions were withering and sensation turning numb.

"I certainly do not. How can you even think of the same. I am more than double your age. Even in the wildest or weirdest of situation, I cannot think of us getting along. Have you ever heard of a love story having teacher-student together? It is dumb and even senseless of you to think of the same," replied Anand out of anguish.

The reply was blunt and to the point. This left Adrija heart-broken and emotionless. Adrija lost her control and filled with anger she backfired, "Then what were those special moments all about? Treating me in a way, like you did to none of your other students. Creating a special environment of warmth around me. Being biased at times and that special hug, when I topped. Were those moments fake?"

Confused, furious and with equal intensity, Anand replied, "You were our academy's most deserving candidate, hence that extra attention. Besides, teachers tend to incline towards their favourite students and turn bit biased over a period. Coming to the hug-thing, if that made you feel like this, then I would like to comment- that your intellect is seriously sub-standard and the IQ even more degraded. I am shocked to know the kind of thoughts filled in your grey matter. This proves nothing, but my ability to fail in recognizing you, as an individual."

Adrija stood disconcerted and suffered a huge setback. She did not know what to talk beyond this and appeared all dud. She had tears rolling down and on facing a flop (in what she misunderstood as a relation), Adrija left without taking the conversation further. Apparently, there was nothing left and all appeared pointless.

On the contrary, Anand appeared disgusted. He felt of Adrija acting immature and the thoughts that she developed, being totally baseless. Anand did not go deep in that phase and wished of not thinking about the conversation anymore. Anand looked at his wrist watch and left. Soon, he called others that had come along and together they left back.

On her way back, Adrija felt cynical and sad. She was very much optimistic on Anand developing the same feeling like hers; but a denial upfront led to the negative impact.

Upon reaching home, Adrija locked herself in the room and wept. She wept the entire night and so wished the entire episode of her being appointed as the class care-taker (the very day Anand received an urgent call in the middle of the test) had not occurred.

However, all said and done, Adrija was not going to keep quiet and that too at least not with the broken-heart.

2017- Adrija's 18th Birthday-

Almost, after a gap of two years from the day of incidence, Adrija called up Anand Sir. She dialed through an unknown number, because of the fear of not picking up through the known one.

As Anand picked up, Adrija said, "Hi Anand Sir. How have you been doing?"

"Adrija?" said Anand out of shock.

"I am glad you recognized my voice. Before calling, I thought you must have forgotten my existence," replied Adrija.

"Why have you called today? And that too suddenly?" asked Anand.

"Yes sir, suddenly, I had to. Please do not disconnect. It is my 18th birthday and you know I have no one to share with," said Adrija and paused.

"I am listening, please continue," replied Anand.

"Oh! By the way, Happy 18th Birthday. God bless you with ample of success and good health. May you get all that you desire and never fall short of smiles. Now, tell me how you ended up calling after such a long time," continued Anand.

"Nothing. Just the need to share this day with someone I look up to and call as mine. As a Guru and friend, though. I will come straight to the point- can you come down to my place for a coffee?" asked Adrija with all hopes.

On not receiving any response from Anand, Adrija continued, "At least this much I deserve sir and that too on a special day like this."

"You very much do and deserve way beyond. I so wish I could give you an affirmative reply, but I have lectures all day. With exams round the corner, taking out time looks extremely difficult. And even you are aware about the drill," replied Anand out of dismay.

"I very well have the knowledge about the process during the exams, but I also know of you taking a lunch break. The duration of the break being two hours, you can very well make it to my house. If not coffee, join me for lunch. Please sir, do not deny" pleaded Adrija.

Anand thought for a while and replied, "Okay. This being your special day, I do not want to dishearten you. I will see you over lunch at 1.30 p.m, but leave soon. You know, I do not wish to miss on my classes."

"Done," replied Adrija happily.

"Cool then, take care. See you," said Anand and kept the call.

Adrija felt glad as she probably found a reason to celebrate her special day. Adrija cooked by herself to further enhance the exclusivity of the meet. All decked up before the special encounter, Adrija waited impatiently of Anand's arrival. Moreover, it was almost after two years, the two were coming together.

As promised, Anand turned up on time and waited outside Adrija's house at 1.30 p.m. He rang the bell and upon hearing the same, Adrija rushed towards the door. On opening the gate, with all gleam on her face and twinkle in the eyes, Adrija said, "I cannot believe your presence sir. So thankful you are here."

"Well, I could not miss out on this special occasion, especially after the invitation by the girl herself, on the very day. Thanks to you for having me here and giving me an opportunity to wish you in person on this very special day. Anyways, Happy 18th Birthday," Anand wished.

Anand gave the bouquet to the girl, he brought along and immediately after the handover, he hugged Adrija. Adrija had not expected the hug. But on receiving the warmth, Adrija felt the same as she did when she was in his arms for the very first time. All the memories from that beautiful encounter came gushing, right in front of Adrija like a flashback.

After exchanging all the warmth, Adrija invited Anand in.

"Please make yourself comfortable sir," said Adrija gesturing Anand to take seat on sofa.

"Some cold drink, juice or lime water to drink? Would you like anything?" asked Adrija out of courtesy.

"No. Thank you. Can we directly proceed for lunch? I need to be back in another hour and you know I cannot be late because there are students waiting, all the time. Also, I am literally starving and do not wish to kill my hunger with these soft drinks," replied Anand with hunger evident from his face.

"Surely, just give me five minutes. I will get the table ready," obliged Adrija and headed straight to the kitchen.

"I have been waiting for this opportunity for almost two years now, and this man seems more bothered about his students waiting at the class. Fine, I assure you, this to be the last lunch of your life and at least my wait coming to an end today," she talked with self and continued to do so, as she added something to glass filled with buttermilk (Anand loved buttermilk post his meal).

Adrija soon took all the cooked meals to the dining hall and kept them over dining table. Once the table was ready, she called Anand sir, "Please come, the food is ready."

Anand could not resist the aroma. Without wasting anytime, he headed towards the table. The food looked delicious and mouthwatering. Glancing on all that was kept on the table, Anand said, "It is your special day and not mine. There was no need to prepare so much. Especially, the efforts that you have put in cooking, these varied delicacies were not required. It appears like some feast. We could have rather ordered from outside or went out for lunch."

"How could I not cook? You have come to my place for the first time and that too on an occasion like this. I could not miss out on serving the best and show you my hospitality. Also, this being your last lunch, it had to be the best," replied Adrija in an affable yet taunting tone.

"Last lunch?" asked Anand out of despair.

"Yaa. We will not be having anymore lunches together after this. You know we do not share any solidarity, so why give any complexity to this simply nothing kind of a relationship," replied Adrija.

She continued to murmur, "You will not have anything ever. This is your last day on my birthday. Good luck!"

"Oh! this way. C'mon not today. No space for grudges on this special day. Come join me for lunch," invited Anand in a jovial tone.

Adrija joined and the two continued to relish the sumptuous food. Anand was bowled over with Adrija's culinary skills and cherished every bite he took.

Upon completing the meal, "I have something that you love," said Adrija.

"My God, there is no space left in my stomach. I have over-eaten and so full, that I might miss out on having anything further for the entire day" replied Anand with a feeling of being overloaded and over-stuffed.

Adrija uncovered (that had hidden behind the big porcelain bowl) the glass filled with buttermilk and handed over the same to Anand. Seeing this Anand immediately said, "I cannot afford to miss on this. And this might in a way help me with digestion."

Anand gulped the entire glass in a jiffy and upon completion said, "Thank you Adrija for the wonderful indulgence. I wish I could stay longer. Sadly, it is time for me to leave."

"Surely it is. And not only leave this house but the world, your fucker. You fucked my life, yet audaciously turned up, over a single call. I am sure you liked me, I know it. I cannot be wrong in understanding my feelings. But I also know, you will never accept the same. You do not care for my feelings and rather care of the societal thoughts. No worries, even I would not regret to what I have done today. Never, ever in my life. Get Lost!" screamed Adrija suddenly losing her cool.

Anand got up on seeing this enflamed side of Adrija and said, "Have you lost it all of a sudden? What is wrong with you? You still seem to have not forgotten that stupid night? I was not inclined by any sense; it is your cooked theory for which I am not to be blamed."

"Oh yes certainly, I am mad. Good I will live with this illusion and you will die with the same. Now get out of my house," and she pushed Anand out with rage.

Anand appeared confused as she mentioned death. However, he did not give much importance to her words, as Adrija had lost control over her mind. Anand continued to drive his way back to the academy and concentrated on his next class.

While here Adrija at her residence, held the bottle in her hands and talked to the same, "Now he will know how love kills." With this as she turned the bottle, the other side had a sticker with POSION written over it.

Not much after long, abruptly in the middle of the class, Anand felt some discomfort in the chest and all of a sudden fell flat on floor. He held his chest tight, began to sweat and found difficult to breathe. One of the students from the class went rushing to call Krishna Kumar (his younger sibling).

Anand's struggle to breathe continued and it increased with every passing moment. There were about 20 odd students but everybody felt helpless and were clueless of providing any sort of assistance in this tough situation. By the time, the kid and Krishna returned, Anand lied lifeless on the floor. Yes, the academy had lost the pioneer Anand Kumar. THE END.

PRESENT DAY- CONVERSATION BETWEEN NAINA & CHANDU IN PROGRESS-

"This is how miserably Anand had an end to his life. In spite of being surrounded by twenty individuals, they could play a role of nothing more than that of mere spectators," said Naina as she finished Anand Kumar's story.

Chandu felt devastated, disturbed and wrecked. He looked clueless on dealing with such disturbing marathon of murder stories. He had come across many individuals as criminals, but Adrija was a psychic. Adrija was one of those, who found pleasure in taking revenge and satiated her soul with gore. Chandu shivered throughout and could not believe of anything that were put in his ears in the last few hours.

"This is all I know and I have helped you to the maximum. Now, as promised you are not going to utter anything about Dheeraj to my dad. Should I trust you on this?" asked Naina out of fear.

"Forget about me telling your dad, I do not even know who you are. I so wished we never met. Me failing on this mission would have been acceptable, but me taking back these horrendous tales (about Adrija) is surely going to give me sleepless nights for long," replied Chandu in a dejected manner.

Naina could not understand what Chandu meant and bamboozled she asked, "What?"

"Nothing! Just leave and do not tell anybody about this encounter. Consider as if this meeting never happened. From now on, you do not know me nor do I ever met you. Did you get that?" asked Chandu as he continued to feel distressed.

"In a way yaa but most of it no," replied Naina still unable to exactly figure out what Chandu meant.

"Good. Leave. And do not turn back once you start walking," instructed Chandu.

Naina felt weird about this man, but as commanded she got up, left and never looked back. Chandu too paid the bill and left.

On getting back to the hotel, Chandu could not wait and dialed Rudra, "Hello, detective Chandu Ray this side."

"Hi Chandu, how are you man? I have been waiting for your call. How is it going?" asked Rudra from the receiving end.

"Do not ask about how is it going and let me tell you- after listening to stories about your beloved Adrija, I am going through terror. What kind of a person are you, man? You have been with Adrija for such a long time and yet unaware of her cold-blooded nature. Consider yourself being lucky, that you are still alive. For a minute before calling, I thought even you must be hung-up in frames (on the wall) and not living anymore," replied Chandu in a wobbling tone.

"What the heck are you speaking, Chandu? Are you drunk? Have you lost it totally?" asked Rudra on not having an iota of an idea of what Chandu meant.

"Forget it. I am leaving tomorrow morning and will reach before noon. I will see you sharp at 4 P. M, at Mohan's Dhaba in Versova. I am sending you the bill, get the money along. Once I give you all the information, I want this case to be closed and never want to meet you, ever again," said Chandu as he continued to feel disgusted.

The dreams of wandering around and exploring Patna never materialized. Chandu was so taken aback by the entire appalling episode, that he left the very next day for Mumbai. Chandu booked an early morning flight, as he continued to feel exorbitant and wanted to emit everything (about Adrija) to the boys at the earliest.

CHAPTER 10

A LIVING NIGHTMARE

Rudra along with a small backpack left the very next morning from Pune to meet Chandu and gather information about Adrija. He appeared normal on the whole but a bit eager from inside, to know what was in store for him. Lesser, did Rudra know that he was going to feel thunderstruck with an upcoming meet with Chandu.

Chandu as scheduled arrived at Mumbai and went straight to his chawl. He relaxed a bit, got fresh and ordered a meal for himself. He still felt nervy and was barely able to forget anything that had been told by Naina. He somehow prayed for the time to pass quickly and desperately waited to meet Rudra.

As the clock struck 4 p.m, Rudra and Chandu both were at the Mohan's Dhaba, Versova. On one hand, where Rudra seemed curious to know the proceedings in the case; Chandu on the other hand appeared wrecked.

Rudra on seating immediately said, "Hey Chandu, so good to see you man. I am happy that you kept your promise and assume of you doing an amazing job."

"Waiter," Chandu on the other hand abruptly called for the waiter.

Rudra felt weird of Chandu's action and waited for him to place the order.

Waiter came and stood next to the table and asked, "Sir your order please?"

"One masala tea for me, with extra ginger and less sugar. And you Rudra?" asked Chandu.

"One chocolate milkshake for me," ordred Rudra.

"Sir anything to munch with the drinks?" asked the Waiter.

To this Chandu replied, "See we have already ordered what we feel like having, just do not interrupt as we talk. As and when our orders are ready, keep it on the table and leave. If we need anything else we would call you for the same. Did you get that?" Chandu had still not forgotten the infringement antics of Adil.

Waiter nodded and left giving strange look to Chandu. Rudra immediately asked, "What was that? Why those special instructions?"

"I do not want him (the waiter) to keep encroaching the serious environment, every time as we share information. Forget, you will not understand as you have not witnessed, all that happened, when I and Naina were in conversation," explained Chandu, although the story did not add any help to Rudra's estranged expressions.

"Can we now come to the point for which this meeting has been held?" asked Rudra, hardly able to suppress his ever escalating curiosity.

"Sure. What else are we here for? So, I went to Patna and met this girl Naina who appears to be a close friend of Adrija," and Chandu paused for sipping in some water.

"And?" asked Rudra, unable to wait.

"And? And …." Chandu shared all the facts and information collected in exact same words and manner. Also, to testify his information Chandu played the recording of his conversation with

Naina.

After hearing the entire story, Rudra was left STUNNED and ANAESTHETIZED. He was unable to find words to comment on the same and was totally dumbfound.

Chandu could very well relate to the situation, as he still continued to suffer the jolts on reminiscing the story. However, leaving behind all the scares, Chadnu said, "I have done my job and this is the bill. Have you got cash or getting it transferred online?"

Rudra still trying to retrieve his system, replied in a very diminished tone, "Online. Provide me with your scanner."

Chandu opened his phone and provided the scanner immediately. Rudra transferred the fee and said, "Can you do one last thing for me?"

"What! No, never, nothing on this case. Take my advice you also forget Adrija, or else you might possibly have an ending similar to those of Kaavya or Anand. She is insane. She neither forgives nor forgets anyone who hurts her," Chandu rebounded and left.

Rudra found himself inept. He was left divided between his mind and heart. His mind constantly cautioned and asked to forget Adrija; whereas his heart (immensely drenched in love) was not ready to give upon Adrija.

Rudra got up, put his backpack and straight headed to Adrija's hostel. Rudra had not informed Adrija about the same, nor did he think of the dire consequences. He just wanted to have a conversation face-to-face and put all qualms to rest.

Rudra traveled for an hour and reached the hostel. At the gate, Bahadur stopped him from getting in, but Rudra continuously necessitated of letting him in. Tired of Rudra's forceful antics, Bahadur after a long hurl called Adrija and said, "Madam, Rudra has come to meet you."

"I am in middle of something, ask him to wait and I shall call him. Just tell him to wait for another 15 or 20 minutes," replied

Adrija over call.

"Madam has asked you to wait for about half an hour. She will call you once she is done with the work," said Bahadur, conveying the message.

Rudra nodded and waited outside the gate, under a bus-stop shade (right next to the hostel gate). After 20 odd minutes Adrija called directly on Rudra's phone and said, "What a pleasant surprise! How come you are here? That too suddenly, without any prior intimation?"

"Let me in, I will tell you everything," replied Rudra in no nonsense manner.

"Okay. You appear as hot as a frying pan. No worries, I will tell Bahadur to allow you in" replied Adrija.

Soon, Rudra was admitted in and he walked his way to the room.

On opening the door, Adrija hugged Rudra. But, Rudra in return responded in a lukewarm mode. Adrija felt the lessened intensity and out of concern asked, "Is everything alright?"

Rudra entered the room, kept his backpack on the bed and opening the front zip of the bag, removed Adrija's personal memoir and said, "This. What is this?"

"Why? Did you not read it? Do you not know what is written inside? When you can take it without telling me, then I am sure you can even read it, without informing!" said Adrija with cynicism.

After glaring at Rudra and a really short pause, she continued, "I came to know of this theft, the very next day when I could not find my diary in the drawer besides my bed. But I just waited so that you could confess and apologize. I did not expect this out of you Rudra."

Rudra felt guilty and fumbled as he spoke, "I did. But I was more shocked when I unearthed the truth."

"What truth?" asked Adrija in dismay.

"The truth behind you killing your mother. The truth of you murdering your professor Anand Kumar and God alone knows what lies beyond this. I did not have the guts to dig furher deep, but I am sure there exists many more facts undiscovered. Am I right Adrija?"

Adrija stood foxed as she heard those past memories making a comeback and that too through Rudra. Moreover, she felt insensate on Rudra discovering these incidents. Adrija had no replies to those questions.

"I am waiting Adrija. And this is not it. But I would like to tell you that your father is no more and you hallucinate his presence" and Rudra threw another deplorable finding at Adrija.

Adrija on hearing the same replied with wrath, "He is not dead and with me all the time. He talks to me and responds whenever I need his help. And what wrong did I do if I killed my mom? You know how and what she was?"

Rudra was stupefied on Adrija's reply, as she still stood in denial on giving upon father-thing. And replying on the latter part Rudra vehemently said, "Your mother was at mistake? Seriously? Your father ill-treated her, yet you have the audacity to justify his wrong-doing? Wow! You seriously need to get yourself checked with the psychiatrist."

"Who are you to take my mother's side and shower sympathy on her. My father was a Hero. He accepted my mother, despite of all her shortcomings. Even after catching her red-handed on having an extra-marital affair, my father did not leave her," replied Adrija as she paused to sip in water.

Without giving Rudra any opportunity to react, Adrija continued with fury, "I agree, my dad misbehaved that night, but that was nowhere close to what she did with him. Also, let me inform you-he started drinking after he was taken aback by her 'so-called' love-life with the other guy. As per logic, my dad should have killed my mom, but he forgave. Talking about my mom, she was any which ways done with the relationship. Hence, killed him over a relatively small scuffle. Therefore, to provide justice to my loving dad I killed my mom, because she refused to surrender. She rather assassinated my dad's character by calling him a drunkard. My mom, told the entire society that he was highly under the influence of alcohol and slipped, resulting in his death."

Rudra melted after hearing Adrija and felt bad for her. But he still did not agree with the latter part of the story of her seeking revenge. To this he replied, "But a life for a life? Is this justice? How could you even try to justify the same?"

"I do not care what you think. I know what I did and I do not have any regrets for the done," replied Adrija ruthlessly.

"Okay and what about killing the professor, Anand Kumar? How would you justify the same?" asked Rudra.

"Well, he used me. I had killed the emotional side of mine after my father's death. He was the one who ignited the flame, but denied upfront on approach. I was still okay with that, but he never looked back until I invited him for my birthday. Look at the audacity of this person, Anand sir unashamedly turned up on a single call; and that too after a span of two years! What would you call I do not know, but I would call Anand sir an opportunist and a coward. Hence, I did what I did," replied Adrija with no guilt in her eyes whatsoever.

Rudra had gone blank by now and understood the cold-blooded nature of Adrija. And tauntingly he asked, "I could only learn about these two facts about you, but are there any more achievements under your name? As in, anymore murders that you would want to justify?"

"I so wished I could kill one more person, my ex. He loved me like you do. He left Patna and went to another city for work-prospect. We did carry on over a long distance relationship for quite some time, but got worse every day (as we all know how difficult it is to carry on these long distance association). And one day we decided to part ways, mutually. But the very next week I came across a social media post of his, posing a cozy picture with a hot chic. I could make out the real reasons behind those bitter brawls," said Adrija with a rage.

Listening to this, Rudra laughed out loud. He held his stomach and rolled on the floor.

Adrija felt bizarre seeing Rudra behave this weird. Rudra rather being serious and/or angry, reacted other way round and kept chuckling. It felt as if Rudra had gone in some shock after hearing such trembling stories and lost sense. After waiting for a while when Rudra did not stop, Adrija out of keenness asked, "What's so funny? Have you totally lost it?"

"So sorry, but I could not control after exploring this- do not dare mess with me, facet of yours. It is commendable. I like this streak of yours, rather madly in love. Moreover, you still wanting to kill another guy, it excites me further. Your unstoppable nature and being on a killing spree excites me. Wow," replied Rudra as he still continued to chuckle.

This confused Adrija to the maximum. The time Rudra entered with dropped-face, conveyed a message of him being unhappy with the killings (but obviously anybody would); exhibiting a different story then and now it appeared something else. On the contrary to the prior hatred, now he appears to be in love with these series of murders.

Rudra laughed even louder on seeing Adrija perplexed and said, "I was right about your eyes, then. They do warn and come with a message- mess at your own risk. I told you on our very first encounter of me searching for a partner. But, lesser did I know, rather never imagined, that I would find a partner with this compatibility ratio. Let me tell you honestly and frankly, this stands way beyond my imagination."

"Rudra stop howling and tell me upfront, what do you mean? Everything appears jumbled up and there are million thoughts running in my mind and that too directionless. I want you to come straight to the point and no more ridiculing please," begged Adrija as she appeared to lose patience.

Rudra stopped laughing and with intense look said, "I am also a cold-blooded ANIMAL like you."

Adrija appeared traumatized and was unable to gulp what she just heard. Gathering all guts, she asked, "C'mon Rudra, stop exaggerating things and tell me with all honesty."

"I mean every bit that I just said," replied Rudra with weightage in his tenor.

Also, it appeared as if Rudra's serious mode got activated. The giggling reverberations had all of a sudden shut and the room echoed with Rudra's intense tone.

"You mean, that you too…. What nonsense! I very well remember you telling me of you being a contractor on our very first date at the café. Stop it Rudra, I am going numb. Please," begged Adrija.

"Yes I am a contractor; I admit of telling you this. But beyond that you did not let me complete and assumed everything on your own," replied Rudra as he maintained the intensity.

"Okay. Usually, contractor is associated with infrastructure related things and I did the same. My mistake. At least now tell me, how you and me are the same?" asked Adrija as she appeared to lose consciousness.

"I am a CONTRACT-KILLER. In our field individuals like me are called CONTRACTOR. I take assignments of contract killing. I do so for money. I know I should have informed you the very day at café. But after seeing you smile and bright, I had no nerves to admit the same," replied Rudra with solemnity and earnestly.

Adrija went blank. She felt all this being a part of karma and which is why she had fallen for a gangster. She could not get out of the relationship, realizing how dangerous the man was. It felt as if she was living a nightmare.

"We will call ourselves as Mr. & Mrs. Serial killers," joked Rudra, to which Adrija just nodded.

"First and foremost we need to see a psychiatrist and get you treated. This hallucination thing is not good for either of us. I hope you do not have any problems with the same," said Rudra in an amplified tone.

"As if I object and you will listen. Do I have a choice?" murmured Adijra.

"Did you say something?" asked Rudra, on not hearing what Adrija replied in an absolute mellowed tone.

"I said, absolutely not. I have no problems," replied Adrija with a fright in her tone.

"Good. So I shall book an appointment with the counsellor and let you know darling. Worry not, we are in this together and should emerge victorious," said Rudra casually.

With this Rudra hugged Adrija and tried making her feel comfortable. Adrija on other hand, felt nothing more than horrified. She had gone pale and blank at the same time.

Although, Rudra instilled hopes, she felt totally hopeless and had no clue about handling the situation. This was a beginning of a new chapter in her life, which was going to be nothing short of an adventurous ride, rather a horrifying one.

CHAPTER 11

THE ENTRY

“May I come in, sir” asked the policeman standing at the door of the cabin.

“Oh yes. Please come in,” replied ACP A. KHAN.

“Thank you Sir,” replied the policeman as he entered the cabin.

“So good to see you. It has been really long. Probably this will be first time ever, that we will we working together, after you joining the police force,” said ACP Khan with a beaming smile on his face.

“For sure sir. I had this opportunity to get trained by you during the academy days, which in itself was no lesser of an achievement. Now finally, would be an honor to work under your leadership,” replied the policeman, as he saluted the ACP.

The compliment had ACP’s chest filed with pride and twirling his moustache with boastfulness Khan said, “Thank you for your kind words. Oh by the way, please have a seat.”

The policeman sat and kept his cap on the table.

“As you know, you have been made part of this elite team on my special request, so I want you have a look at this file. I would want to know your take on the case,” said Khan as he pushed the case file towards the cop.

He picked up the file and began to read. With every page turned, the intensity of the expressions amplified; and how serious the case was, became evident from his facial lexes.

"Sir what is this?" asked the cop in utmost disbelief on pointing at the fact which read- more than 47 people murdered so far.

"Go on and complete the case file," instructed ACP Khan.

The policeman continued to scan the file and the facts surfacing in the upcoming pages, made him even more restless. By the end of the file, he had understood the urgency of the matter and the reason why he was here.

"Sir, let's go for the kill. He has been aided so far by big politicians and other powerful people. This is the same reason why we do not have any substantial evidence against him. The cover has never been blown, but now is the time to get this bastard behind the bars," said the policeman as he finished inspecting the file.

"I expected nothing less than this reaction. So, go ahead and get rolling. It is ACTION time!" replied Khan with fierce.

The policeman got up from his seat, wore his cap and with intense strut said, "I assure you sir, nothing short of success. Soon, Rudra will be in our custody and serving the desired sentence."

"Surely. Your success in the last case (Sayyed-Ul-Haq) has increased my anticipations and reached SKY-HIGH. I would expect no less of an intensity, with which you and your team worked in the nationwide catastrophe. So, Mr. RANBIR KHANDELWAL, welcome to the team and now you are in charge of the operation 'HUNT THE HUNTER'. Please leave and start working on the assignment with immediate effect," ordered ACP Khan with severity in his tone.

Ranbir saluted the ACP and left. He was just given charge of his next mission and Ranbir appeared raring to go. With 'HUNT THE HUNTER', Ranbir planned to go all in and GO FOR THE KILL.

On one hand where Rudra had plans of settling down and went

mad behind Adrija; on the other Ranbir had plans of nabbing the man and see him in the jail. An absolute thrill-seeking (not so love) TRIANGLE, was on the cards.

THE END

that awaits A NEW BEGINNING...

9 789393 262806